Return to Aadya
Book Two of The Sisters of Aadya

by Leigh Titler

DORRANCE
PUBLISHING CO
EST. 1920
PITTSBURGH, PENNSYLVANIA 15238

Dorrance Publishing Co
585 Alpha Drive
Pittsburgh, PA 15238
Visit our website at dorrancebookstore.com

ISBN: 978-1-6366-1492-2
eISBN: 978-1-6366-1671-1

Dedications

This book is dedicated to Adrienne NaDell Crampton and Michelle Scott. Adrienne has been many things for me, friend, sister, a shoulder to cry on and in this set of books you are my Acelyn. Michelle, you have been many things to me as well, friend, sister, and my tether to reality when I would drift too far into the darkness; and in this set of books you are my Zanderley. I count my blessings every day knowing that I have you both in my life. You two have made me a better person just for knowing both of you. I am looking forward to many more years with you both. No one knows what the future holds for us. So, here is to many more trips around the sun. I love you both!

Prologue

In their potions room, Kane and Catarina watched the heroes make their plans. "Kane," she said with tears in her eyes.

"What is it, my love? Why all the tears?"

"Oh, it is nothing, I am just emotional. The princesses have come so far already. But they still have so far to go," she said wiping away a stray tear.

Walking over to stand behind her, he looked over into the mirror while massaging her shoulders. "I know they will win this war," he said leaning over and kissing the back of her head. As they watched in silence, Catarina relaxed into Kane's embrace. Out of the silence a loud boom rattled the castle walls. Jumping out of his embrace, she turned to look at him.

"Kane! What was that?" asked Catarina with wide and startled eyes.

Just then a little woodland gnome knocked franticly and yelling "Miss Cat, Miss Cat we have a problem please let me in!"

Rushing to the door, she threw it open making the gnome fall into the room and forcing him to wrap his arms around her legs. Bending down and embracing the little guy, she spoke softly to try and calm him down. "What is wrong, little one?"

Still shaking like a leaf, he looked up at her and said, "Morgana is here."

With a wave of his hand, Kane changed the vision in the mirror showing the outside of the castle walls. "Darling, you need to flee the castle. Morgana has broken through the cloaking spell that had the castle hidden," said Kane looking back at Catarina.

"What about you, my love?" asked Catarina.

"I will flee as well but I am going to distract her so you can slip away."

"No, I will not leave you alone."

Bending down, Kane spoke to the little gnome, "Go now! Escape through the tunnels in the back of the castle, meet up with us where the Sisters of Fate sleep." Nodding, the little gnome ran off. Looking at Catarina he cupped her face, "You must go, I will be fine. I will meet up with you at our meeting spot. You must protect the child you are carrying." With a smile, he leaned in and kissed her. Her face softened as she placed a hand on her stomach and with a sniffle she nodded. Leaning in, she kissed him and praying to the gods that it would not be their last. They stood and with a wave of his hand his human form faded away and in its place was a falcon that hovered just for a moment and flew off. Looking around quickly to make sure she did not need anything, she crouched, let out a cry, and she shifted into a black cat. Jumping onto the table that held the mirror she pawed at it three times, the vision shimmered, and she jumped through. Once the ripples stopped, the mirror went black and shattered.

Chapter One

Sitting at the table under the pergola, Acelyn sat and observed everyone who had come into her life recently. Looking over at Jaz the brave little dragon that if it were not for him, they all would have died. Then there is Jewel, the little pixie. She smiled and shook her head; she watched her flutter up and down in the middle of the table. Coda, one of the mighty dragon guardians. He has such sad eyes, the guilt must way on him over Zanderley. Oh, and we cannot forget Anton. Acelyn studied him, she liked how his eyes lit up when he was joking around with the other guardians. Or how his face took on a dark look when Temprance and Acelyn were about to do something he did not feel comfortable with. He must have felt her eyes on him. He turned his head slowly and looked at her. She swore his eyes could see right into her soul; Acelyn could not handle the intense look he was giving her, so she looked away quickly and settled on Temprance. Temprance is beautiful, smart, brave everything Acelyn wished she could be. As Acelyn sat and watched her sister interact with Zeke, her soul mate. Who would have thought that she would find her mate for life so soon? Acelyn's heart yearned for what Temprance had found with Zeke, the way they look at each other like there is no one else on earth.

"Acelyn. Hello, come back from daydream land," said Jewel waving her hands franticly in front of her face.

Coming out of a daze, Acelyn blinked, "What?"

"Princess, are you even listening?" asked Jewel landing in front of her with her hands on her hips.

1

With cheeks turning pink from embarrassment from being caught daydreaming she shook her head, "Sorry, Jewel, I was caught in my own thoughts."

Flying up, she kissed Acelyn's cheek, "It is okay. I know all of this is a lot to take in," waving her hand at the table.

With a look of concern on her face, "Hey, Ace, you, all right? Do you need a time out to collect your thoughts?" asked Temprance.

With a shake of her head "Naw, Tempie, I'm good. Let us figure out how to get our sister then save our aunt."

"Okay, let us work this out. Jewel, where did you say our Zanderley was again?" asked Temprance.

Flying to the center of the table, she landed on top of a bowl full of fruit, "She is in Athens, Greece."

"Well, that's a little bit of a pickle," said Acelyn.

All at once everyone turned and looked at her. Scratching his head Anton leaned over and asked, "What does that mean?"

Forgetting the only one who would know what she was talking about would be Temprance, so she explained to everyone, "It means that is a little bit of a problem."

Not quite understanding, "Why would that be a problem? We will just go there," said Anton.

Rolling her eyes, she stood up and walked around the table and placed her hands on Temprance's shoulders. "Because my sister is uncomfortable about flying and that is the only way we will get there."

Reaching up she laid her hand on Acelyn's. "Thanks sis, but we will be on an airplane. I should be okay."

Giving her shoulders a squeeze, "That's all fine. I am sure we have our passports, but the rest don't, and how do you suggest we get four dragons and a pixie on a plane? If the guys freak out and shift, we will crash. If Jaz or Jewel shift, it will give the people on the plane a show and upset the balance."

Anton spoke up "I have a suggestion." All eyes were on him now, "What if we fly like we did to come here? That way Temprance would feel a little more comfortable."

While everyone was debating on the pros and cons of flying both ways, the tiny pixie grew terribly upset. No one would listen to her, finally she was so mad she felt as if she were on fire. She felt the fire grow from within her stomach not noticing wherever she was stomping she was leaving fiery footprints behind her.

"What is burning?" asked Acelyn. Looking down she saw the stomping pixie. Tapping her sister "What's up, Ace?" Taking her hand and turning her sister's head towards Jewel, everyone stopped moving. The little pixie was stomping around and complaining. "Go help the girls his note said, you will be doing a great service he said, but how can I help if no one listens to me!" When she stomped both of her feet flames engulfed her and then she was gone.

Jumping up from her seat and knocking Acelyn over, "What the hell, she went poof!" Looking around to see if she could find any trace of Jewel, "Where did she go?" asked Temprance.

Picking herself up off the ground she bent over and looked under the table, "Well she is not under here." said Acelyn.

The only one not moving or saying anything was Jaz. "Hey Jaz, do you see her?" asked Anton.

"What the hell!" said Acelyn when she noticed Jaz went as still as stone. Walking over to him she crouched so she could look at him in the eyes, "Jaz, what is it?"

Shaking his head, Jaz looked at Acelyn with wide eyes. "It cannot be," he said quietly.

Walking over to join them Temprance crouched on the other side and laid her hand on his arm. "Acelyn, I have never seen him like this, is he okay?" asked Temprance.

"Tempie, I have no idea, he has been like this since she went poof," said Acelyn while rubbing his arm and looking at her sister.

"Has he said anything?" asked Zeke.

"Yes, he said 'It cannot be.' Does anyone know what he meant by that?" asked Acelyn looking at Zeke, Coda, and Anton.

"I think he is in shock," said Temprance.

"Well, what do we do?" asked Acelyn "We just can't leave him like this."

While the others tried to bring Jaz out of his state of shock, the little pixie cowered and shook like a leaf, because in front of her stood four spirits of dragon guardians. The red dragon lowered his head and spoke softly. "Little dragon pixie, there is no reason to be scared, what is your name little one?"

But Jewel did not move, thinking to herself, "Oh dang nab it how do I always get in these messes? Why is he calling me a dragon pixie, they have been gone for centuries? Maybe if I do not move, they will go away and forget about me." Tucking herself tighter into a ball, she noticed something not quite right. She had a tail. Opening her eyes, she noticed her skin was not skin anymore. Somehow her skin had erupted into scales. Freaking out and forgetting about the spirit guardians, she jumped up and ran in a circle chasing her tail. "Oh, shit how did this happen? What kind of sick joke are the gods playing on me now?"

Stepping forward, the great white spirit dragon spoke up. "Little dragon pixie, please calm down and we will explain." Jewel skidded to a stop and looked up. "That is a good girl. Now come here and we will tell you what has happened."

Looking down Jewel noticed that she not only had a tail and scales she was a freaking dragon. Her scales were black and purple, her body was black, the underbelly and wings were the same color of her favorite deep purple irises, and the inside of her wings were a violet color. Looking up with tears in her eyes, "What happened to me?" is what she meant to say but all that came out were purple and black flames. Startled she scuffled backwards and collapsed, weeping she pulled her wings over her head so that they would not see her cry.

She felt a snout nudge her wing, opening just a little all she could see was the face of the white dragon. "Little one my name is Galaxy, I will not hurt you, please come out." Opening her wings Jewel studied her, she was not just white. She had blue, purple, and pink scales and the wings at the tips were feathers. Looking down quickly she noticed she had feathers on the tips of her wings as well. Leaning down Galaxy placed her snout on top of Jewel's head.

Jewel felt the change take over her, she faded out, and then she was normal again but just a little different. She was in human form, but she was adult size and was wearing a white flowing gown. Spinning in a circle like she was chasing her tail she noticed her hair was past her waist. Looking up to Galaxy she asked, "What happened to me?"

Like magic all the dragons shifted into humans. Jewel took a startled step back. "Oh no, do not be scared little one, we will not hurt you we are here to help. What is your name?"

Taking a shaky breath, she stepped forward, "My name is Jewel."

With a warm smile Galaxy said, "Hello, Jewel, it is nice to meet you. My name is Galaxy, and they are," pointing at the others, "Blaze, the red and black one, Ursula, the blue and black, and last but not least that is Emery, the green and black."

"What are you? You are not like other dragons; your wings are different."

With a soft laugh Galaxy nodded. "We are the spirits of dragon pixies."

With wide eyes, "What? They really exist?"

"Yes, Jewel, they do. You, my child, are a dragon pixie."

Shaking her head, "You must be mistaken," said Jewel. "I cannot be a dragon pixie. I would have known, plus I would have had my powers a long time ago."

"Your powers were suppressed so that Morgana and Kahn would not find out about you. If they knew what you were, they could have drained you dry," said Blaze.

"So why now? Do you not think we have enough problems on our plates without throwing this in the mix?" Jewel said bitterly.

"Once you learn how to use your new powers, you will be able to help the princesses more. Now you must return to the princesses; they are frantic not knowing what happened to you."

"How am I to help them? We cannot even get to where Kahn has Zanderley."

"My suggestion is to slip them in and out of the realms," said Emery.

Tapping her lips with her finger Galaxy nodded, "I agree, portal hopping is going to be the best bet. Now go. We will see each other soon."

Just as fast as they arrived, they were gone. For the first time she looked around at her surroundings. There were white pillars, turning, she counted them. "Twelve pillars," looking up there was a throne on top of each pillar. She wanted to get a closer look so when she tried to turn back into a pixie, nothing happened. "Oh, come on, this sucks monkey farts, I am going to miss my wings," then she felt something flitter behind her. She had wings, much bigger wings but she had wings. Getting excited she wiggled her wings and rose off the ground flying up so she could see, her hand flew to her mouth and she gasped.

Chapter Two

As Jewel studied each one of the thrones, she noticed each one had a stone etching on their high backs. There was a thunderbolt, peacock, trident, fire, owl, vulture, sun, moon, winged helmet, a dove, a hearth, and a Cerberus. As much as she tried not to, she said each one out loud and touched each symbol as she went. On the first one she traced the thunderbolt "Zeus, Hara, Poseidon, Hephaestus, Athena, Ares, Apollo, Artemis, Hermes, Aphrodite, Hestia, and Hades. Flying back to the center of the room she spun, "Oh my, I am in the throne room of the Olympian Twelve," she said quietly.

Jewel was too immersed in looking at the stone carvings to notice she was no longer alone. Artemis found herself very entertained watching the floating creature. After about ten minutes the goddess spoke, "Is there something I can help you with, my dear?"

Letting out a shriek that could shatter glass, Jewel flew and hid behind Artemis's throne, peeking around the side to see who spoke to her. Looking around she saw nothing, confused she came out from her hiding spot. Then once again the voice came from behind her, "No need to be frightened I will not bite." Before she could fly off Artemis grabbed the back of her dress. "Settle down!"

With arms and legs flailing she yelled, "Do not kill me. I mean no harm. Please let me go."

With a burst of laughter Artemis pulled Jewel back and sat her in a throne, once she felt her back hit the throne Jewel covered her face with her hands.

7

"What is your name?" asked Artemis.

Peeking through her fingers she stilled the sight before her. Artemis reached up and pulled Jewel's hands off her face one by one.

Speaking slowly Jewel asked, "Are you a God?"

"Yes, my tiny friend, I am Artemis and who are you?"

"Me am Jewel, I mean my name is Jewel."

"I am going to let you go, please do not run."

Jewel nodded slowly as Artemis let go of her arm. "Please do not be mad at me I did not mean any harm," apologized Jewel.

"No need to apologize, you did nothing wrong. I am just wondering why you summoned me here?"

"Me!" Pointing to herself, shaking her head franticly "I did not summon you."

"You must have, there is no one else here. By any chance did you touch the symbols on the thrones?" asked Artemis.

Hanging her head knowing what she did wrong she nodded.

"No need to be ashamed, Jewel," she said while placing a finger under Jewel's chin and lifting it to look into her eyes. "It was just a question, like I said before you did no wrong. Well since I am here is there anything, I can do for you?" she said with a smile.

"Yes, I have new powers and I do not know how to use them. Can you teach me?"

As Jewel looked up into Artemis's eyes, she had the weirdest feeling come over her, she felt calm and excited all at once. The longer she studied Artemis the more enthralled she became. Artemis was a true beauty. She has long sable brown hair, her skin is flawless like a porcelain doll. She could not look away from her eyes they were white and had electricity running through them. Every time they sparked Jewel could feel the power radiate from Artemis in waves. Artemis is wearing this beautiful sheer two-piece white outfit that was transparent, the top part was just enough to cover her breasts, her stomach was bare, and the skirt was floor length with a slit up to her hip where there was only a leather strap that tied it closed.

Jewel could hear someone talking but it sounded like it was in the far distance. She felt warmth on her shoulder then spread throughout her whole body. Blinking slowly Jewel came back to reality. "Huh, what happened?"

With a chuckle, Artemis took her hand from Jewel's shoulder. "You went into a trance, my little friend."

"What, how did that happen?" asked Jewel.

"It will happen if you look a God or a Goddess in the eyes for too long," explained Artemis.

"Now, how are any of us going to be able to talk with any of you if that happens?" said Jewel in a huff with her hands on her hips.

Artemis tipped her head back and laughed. Then she closed her eyes and when she opened them, they were a brilliant shade of blue. "This should help, my tiny friend."

"Wow, you can just change your eye color by blinking?" asked Jewel.

"Yes, we can also disguise ourselves to where we look like another person. Now little one, what can I do to help you?"

"I need to figure out how to control my new powers. I don't even know where to start."

"Answer me this, when you used your powers before where did you feel them come from?"

Jewel took a minute to think. "Well, I would feel warmth come from my belly," explained Jewel.

"Okay, so your magic still comes from the same place as it did before. You are a dragon pixie. So, your magic comes from the flame you hold inside of you. Now I want you to transform into your dragon form."

"I do not know how," said Jewel feeling defeated.

"Of course, you do, all you need to know is in your heart. Now close your eyes and concentrate."

Letting out a huff, Jewel closed her eyes and pictured herself as a dragon. Jewel felt her tail grow and her arms and legs lengthen. The sound of bones shifting and cracking filled the throne room. Jewel's vision went red from pain when her horns sprouted from her head. Then her body erupted into scales. She let out a roar that caused purple and black flames to burst out of her mouth when her wings grew from her back. Shaking and utterly exhausted from her transformation, her legs gave out and she collapsed.

Artemis walked over to where Jewel was laying on the floor. Crouching down, she stroked Jewel's jaw and the top of her head. "See, there you go my tiny friend, you did it. Now next time will not hurt as badly; once you get used to changing, it will not hurt at all. Now once you catch your breath and gain your strength back, turn back into your human form."

Jewel snorted in response sending purple and black puffs of smoke to come from her nostrils. "You know, Jewel, you are very beautiful in your dragon form." Artemis ran a hand down Jewel's feathered wings, "the colors of purple and black in your feathers mean you descend from royalty and they are so soft."

Jewel lifted her head and looked back at Artemis and just blinked. Jewel let out a yawn and shook her head. She went very still, her form started to shimmer and fade, the dragon disappeared and in its wake was Jewel's human form. "Artemis that really hurt," said Jewel.

Lifting her hand to cup Jewel's cheek her eyes softened, "I know sweetheart, but I promise it will not be so bad next time," said Artemis with a warm smile.

"Artemis, can I ask you a question?"

"Of course, you may ask me anything."

"Why did you have me start with my dragon form?"

"Because that will be the hardest thing for you to learn. Now it is time for me to get back to Mount Olympus. If you need me all you need to do is call for me, and if I am able, I will come to help you. I will let my brother know so he can keep an ear open for calls for help as well. He has been meddling in this mess helping the Princesses. So, until then my small friend, take care and may you go with the speed of the gods."

Jewel watched her fade away then got slowly to her feet and took one last look around the great throne room to the Gods. Then she closed her eyes and pictured a portal to where Temprance and Acelyn were. She felt the warmth deep in her belly and then it started to grow. When she opened her eyes, she saw a portal and on the other side was Temprance, Acelyn, and the others still at the table under the pergola. Letting out a sigh of relief, she smiled and walked through the portal.

Chapter Three

As Jewel was just making it back to her friends, they were all unaware that they were being watched by Morgana. "So, there is still a dragon pixie who survived the curse. Well, she will be my first target. I want her power, and to make it all the sweeter she is from royal blood. With her blood alone it will feed my power for years." She looked down at her loyal companion and pet one of his heads "Now my good boy, I want you to go get me that pixie. But do not hurt a hair on her head, I need her alive. Now go and do not disappoint me," said Morgana with a hiss.

Back in Edan, time seemed to stand still when Jewel walked through the portal.

With wide eyes and pointing at Jewel, "Holy crap she grew up, and what the hell happened to you? Where did you go? Are you okay?" Putting her hands on her hips and slashing her eyebrows down, she started to scold Jewel. "You worried the hell out of us. Jaz has been speechless; the guys have searched everywhere for you. Oh, and you are not allowed to go poof anymore. Do you understand me? And what do you have to say for yourself?" Acelyn hollered.

Jewel stood there not being able to speak from seeing the worry and love in all her new friends' faces. Knowing that she needed to say something she did the only thing she could think of; she lifted her hand to wave and squeaked out, "Hi guys."

Stunned, all the others could do was stare, then suddenly, they all started talking at once bombarding her with questions. "What happened to you?" "Where did you go?" "How did you get so big?" "Where did you come from?"

"Where you hiding somewhere?" "You are a dragon pixie!" Out of all the chaos and yelling she heard the softest voice. Even though it was the softest voice, it sounded loud and clear. She turned her head and gave a little smile to Jaz. Returning her smile, he walked over to her and just gazed into her eyes. Jaz lifted his hands and cupped her cheeks and speaking just as soft as he did the first time he said, "I have found you. I have had dreams about you."

The electric shock that was created when Jaz cradled her cheeks in his hands made her take a deep breath. She was so consumed by what was happening between her and Jaz she did not realize that she had frozen time. Jaz noticed there was no noise, no one yelling. Looking around, he saw Zeke standing behind Temprance with is hands on her shoulders. Temprance was looking over at Jewel and pointing. Anton had his arms around Acelyn's waist, Acelyn looked like she was trying to fly over the table at Jewel. Coda was still sitting at the table with his eyes closed and hands over his ears.

Looking back at Jewel he spoke, "Um, I think you froze them, my fiery beauty." Then he took a closer look, she was not breathing. Jewel's cheeks were starting to look pink from holding her breath for too long. "Jewel, you need to breathe; you are going to pass out." Jewel opened her eyes and looked at Jaz for the first time since he had touched her, she noticed he was still touching her. She looked over at the others frozen in time and slowly exhaled. As Jewel exhaled, she noticed her friends started to move once again. It was like someone had put the world on pause and hit play but in slow motion.

Once everything seems to be back to normal, she took two giant steps and backed out of Jaz's touch. "I just need a little distance. I have had so much thrown at me in such a short time and then there is you, and it is just too much too quick." She said with a soft warm smile. Raising her voice, she yelled so the others could hear her. "Quiet everyone!" All the yelling just stopped. "There that seemed to work, now if you would all sit down, I have a little show and tell for everyone," said Jewel with the biggest smile that she has ever had.

It took a couple of hours, but once Jewel was done no one said a word for what seemed a good ten minutes. Acelyn was the first to talk, "So you are telling me that you met a Greek God?"

"Jewel has been missing for four hours and that is the first question you ask?" asked Anton.

"Yes, stick in the mud, that is the first thing I asked. Remember I grew up in Edan so all the stories we have heard about the Greek Gods and Goddesses are all considered as myths," said Acelyn with her hands on her hips and sticking her tongue out at him.

This sent everyone into a fit of laughter even Acelyn. Jewel could not shake the feeling that she was being watched. She shivered involuntary but it would not stop the feeling of someone putting an ice pick between her shoulder blades.

"Umm Jewelzie, are you okay?" asked Acelyn.

Jewel put a finger up to her mouth "Shhh!" Just then her defenses kicked in, she let out a loud scream and her human form faded away. Jewel twitched her tail and caught the table and sent it flying into the side of the house. When it hit, the table splintered into a million pieces. She tipped her head back and roared sending black and purple flame to just miss the top of the trees. The heat from the flames was just hot enough to scorch just the tips of the leaves, turning them black. She lowered her head and opened her wings to protect the others when she heard a low insidious growl.

Orthrus came from the shadows, he stalked towards Jewel with only one thing in mind. He must capture her, for if he did a good job maybe his master would reward him. Morgana's words kept playing on in his head, "Do not kill her, I want her back here alive. Do you understand me? Remember Orthrus, if you kill her, I will bring you pain, you will wish you were dead. Now go!"

"What the hell is that?" yelled Acelyn. Stepping in front of her, "That my dear would be Orthrus, Morgana's pet Cerberus," said Anton. Acelyn watched the black three-headed dog as it crept closer. All three heads were snarling and the drool that dripped from its mouths was a yellowish color and when it hit the ground it killed the grass.

"Look its drool even kills the grass, how are we going to fight something like that?" asked Acelyn.

"Sis, do you know what a Cerberus is?"

Rolling her eyes "Yeah, that thing!" said Acelyn pointing at Orthrus.

"Yes Ace, but they are also known as Hell Hounds, to serve the Lord of the Underworld, Hades. The first hell hound was named Cerberus and was Hades lap dog. Cerberus was defeated by Hercules and thrown back into the underworld so he could die at his master's feet. But no one knew at the time that Cerberus had mated with a female and had two pups. This must be one of the pups. They say that a bite from any of the heads of a Cerberus will leave you to die a slow and agonizing death because their saliva is made up of sulfur and acid. Their bodies are as strong as a bear and their tail is of a serpent and more deadly than a viper's bite."

"Tempie, how in the world do you know all of this?" asked Acelyn.

"I have always loved Greek mythology, even growing up I obsessed over it. Tessa would buy me books and pictures so I could decorate my room."

"Um, ladies, I am glad you think we have time for a history lesson and bond, but we have other things more important to deal with. Like this huge hell hound to be exact," scolded Anton.

The girls turned their heads and looked toward Jewel and noticed that her soft feathers that are on her wings had hardened into armor. Jewel's scales had changed colors, she was now a dark slate gray with black horns and black wings. Her tail grew spikes on the end that looked sharp as razors.

Backing up, "What happened to our tiny friend?" the girls said in unison.

"She looks scary!" said Temprance.

"No, she looks bad ass!" said all three of the guys in unison.

"No, she's beautiful." Said Jaz walking up beside her placing his hand on her right flank.

Jewel pawed the ground with her right front foot and her claws scarred the earth. As Orthrus came closer she snorted sending pitch black smoke into the air. Worried that Jaz was too close, she took her hind leg and kicked him back behind her for safety. Once Orthrus was close enough, she reared back on her hind legs and came down on top of him sinking her claws into his body causing the hell hound to scream out in pain. The blood that came from his wounds flowed like molten lava and set the grass on fire when it hit the ground. Lowering her head, Jewel bit the middle head's neck and ripped it from the body. But as soon as the head was ripped off it started to grow back. The left head was able to sink its teeth into Jewel's neck. Jewel let out a roar that shook the ground, when she cried out in pain Jaz let out a battle cry and shifted. Taking flight, he looked down onto the fight and aimed for the ground letting his claws and teeth sink in to Orthrus when he landed. Looking back at the girls, "Stay put do not try and help. You do not have any defenses against his bite or from his tail. You still do not have all your powers yet. So please listen to me and stay safe," said Anton before shifting with the other two and joining the fight.

As Temprance and Acelyn watched the dragons try and tear apart Orthrus they felt helpless. The dragons were ripping him from limb to limb but as fast as they would tear something off it would just grow back. Acelyn grabbed Temprance's arm to stop her from running over to Zeke when the snake on the tale sunk into his neck.

"Ace, I just can't stand here and let the man I love and my new family fight to the death."

"Maybe we don't have to," said Acelyn.

"What do you mean, how can we help if we can't join the fight?" asked a frustrated Temperance.

"Tempie, Anton said that we couldn't move from this spot. But he never said we could not join the fight. Remember we are more than just shifters we also have magic."

"Okay, what do you suggest?"

"You are the one that knows Greek mythology what is that things weakness?"

"From what I remember I think their weakness is their heart. But we cannot get close enough to stab it in the heart. Remember, we can't move from here."

Acelyn thought for a second, "I have an idea, take my hand," said Acelyn holding her hand out to her sister.

Once Temprance grabbed Acelyn's hand, she looked at Temprance "Now close your eyes and picture a sword made of ice."

As the girls concentrated, the sky grew dark with storm clouds and the wind picked up. There was almost a winter's bite to the wind, Temprance peeked open one eye and the sight she saw made her breath hitch in her chest. In front of the girls was a swirl of snow, water, ice, and wind making a small vortex. Not wanting to say anything she tugged on her sister's hand to make her open her eyes. Acelyn let out a small gasp as the wind died down and what had been left in its wake. There hovering in midair was a double-edged short sword with beautiful sapphires on the hilt.

"Ace, we did it, but now what do we do with it?" asked Temprance.

"Now we say a spell and send it into that beast's chest and send it back to hell."

Acelyn tightened her grip on Temprance's hand and closed her eyes and began to chant.

Oh, Hail to the Gods and Goddesses
Please hear our plea.
Send this sword with aim and grace

Into the heart of the beast to freeze its fiery heart
and send it straight back to hell
so, mote it be

As soon as Acelyn was done speaking, the sword twisted and turned then flew true, straight into Orthrus's heart. He let out a scream that was almost human. His eyes were the first to die, the flames that burned a deep crimson red turned blue before winking out. Then little by little his whole body turned to ice. Once his body was incased in ice, the girls ran over to the group. Acelyn reached down and grasped the hilt of the sword and slid it out of Orthrus's dead body. Once the sword was out, Temprance turned and gave Orthrus's body a kick shattering him in to a million pieces. When they landed, they melted into the ground putting out the flames his blood had started in the battle and leaving no trace of the beast.

Looking down at the sword in her hand she noticed the see-through ice sword turned to titanium and on the hilt of the short sword along with the sapphires was her name, Acelyn Queen of Aadya.

Chapter Four

Acelyn looked up to get her sister's attention and noticed all the guys still in dragon form bowing to Jewel. Their front legs bent, head tipped down, and wings fully extended. It was such a beautiful sight to see. Jewel's scales and colors had turned back to normal. Acelyn looked over at Temprance and noticed she was kneeling next to Zeke and had her head bowed as well. So Acelyn slowly walked over to Anton and placed her hand on his shoulder and heard his voice loud and clear for the first time.

"Please bow, my love, and show my Queen you respect her." Without arguing Acelyn dropped to one knee and bowed her head. Minutes passed then they all heard a voice that made them bust up laughing. "What the hell are you crazy people doing? Stand up, there is no reason to bow."

Slowly the dragons lifted their heads and shifted back to their human forms. "Please forgive us, Your Majesty, but we were just giving you the respect you deserve," said Anton boldly.

"What do you mean? I am not a Queen I am just the same Jewel that you met a week ago. The only thing that has changed is that my human form is bigger, and I have new powers," explained Jewel.

Anton stood and took a step forward before speaking, "Jewel, you are a dragon pixie and by the color of your scales and feathers you are of royal blood. Also, with you being able to change your whole appearance and it being battle armor you are the daughter of the legendary king and queen of the dragons," explained Anton.

"But all the dragon races have their own king and queen. You must not know what you speak of." Jewel said with a huff.

"Come on guys lets go sit down somewhere, Jewel looks like she could faint," said Acelyn.

As they all gathered in the house none of them noticed the storm that was about to rage outside. When they were all comfy in the living room Temprance jumped up, "Hold off on telling your story, Anton, I am going to go make us some tea."

"I am going to go help by getting us something to eat as well," said Acelyn.

In the kitchen, Temprance studied her sister even though they have not known each other for very long, she could tell there was something bugging her.

"Hey Sis, what's eaten' ya?"

"Just a bunch of stuff on my mind, I guess."

Acelyn took a minute to gather her thoughts then she turned and looked at her sister. "I am worried about Zanderley and Aunt Bella. Also, I am just a little scared of Jewel now. But most of all, I am starting to get feelings for Anton."

"Okay let us take this one problem at a time. First, our sister and aunt will be fine because we are going to save them. Two, Jewel is right, she is still the same person she was before she disappeared. Yeah she might be a queen now and have more powers, but she is still the same sweet pixie. Three, your feelings for Anton, I say don't fight them let them grow and see where it takes you."

"Temprance, get real, this is not the time to 'just let us see what happens.' We have too much other stuff to be worried about than if I have a love connection with an arrogant, bossy dragon," said Acelyn with a huff while cutting the cherry tomatoes with a little extra force.

Letting out a little giggle, Temprance walked over to her sister and placed her hands on her shoulder and turned Acelyn to face her. "Acelyn, sweetheart, it sounds like he has already gotten under your skin."

"Well, I am glad this amuses you. So, what if he has, all I have to do is stay away from him."

"Oh, yeah that will really work when we have to work with them to save our realm," said Temprance with a smug smile.

"Oh, shut up, you ass," said Acelyn turning out of her sister's grasp to put the finishing touches on their food. Grabbing the tray of sandwiches and plate of cherry tomatoes with mozzarella and basil, she stomped out of the kitchen to join the others in the living room. Temprance grabbed glasses and the pitcher of tea she made. It was garnished with lemon, chamomile, and mint. She walked with a little more pep in her step knowing her sister would soon feel what it is like, to share a soul with someone that loves you as much as you love them.

Once everyone was settled in the living room, Anton started his story. "Over one hundred years ago there was only one king and queen of the dragons. The king of the dragons was Obsidian. Yes, Zeke, your father was named after him. The queen was named Opal. The Fates said that they would only be granted one child, once that child was born, she must be hidden with the keeper." Jewel whispered, "Draco." "Yes, Jewel, he was charged to keep you safe and away from the wars. You see years ago when your parents were killed, it was Morgana who killed them. When Morgana thought she killed and drained the magic from all dragon pixies, she went back to her hide out. So, to keep you safe the dragon factions had a meeting. The decision they came up with was you were to stay hidden and your powers bound. Then once you were ready you could take the throne back. Then they put their plan in effect, each faction would have their own king and queen until you came back and took your place next to the sisters," explained Anton waving his hand at Temprance and Acelyn.

Jewel sat back and let out a breath she did not know she was holding. "So, what do I do now?" she asked

"Well, I suggest you do what we are doing just take it one day at a time. Jewel, you are not alone we will be here to help you along the way, just like you have been here for us," said Temprance reaching over and placing her hand on Jewel's.

"Well, I think we need to take a time out and just process what has happened today. Jewel has had an eventful day so far. Then after we eat dinner, we will figure out what we need to do next to save our sister," said Acelyn, while picking up the plates and cups from their lunch.

Everyone went their own way; Jaz went with Jewel to try and help her get a handle on her new powers. Temprance and Zeke decided to go swimming in the pool and Acelyn went to the kitchen to clean up and figure out what to cook this army of banned heroes for dinner. Thinking she was alone she put in her earbuds and set her iPod on shuffle and started to dance while cleaning.

That is how Anton found her twenty minutes later. Leaning up against the counter he studied her, trying to figure out why she was his soul mate and not someone else. But the more he watched the more he was enchanted by her. Her beautiful emerald green eyes sparkled and danced when she laughed or smiled, or the way her hair moved when her hips swayed when she moved. He could still feel her hair and how soft it was against his scales when she almost died. How complete he felt when he held her while they all waited for her to wake up. He never noticed that he left the counter and was walking over to her. Acelyn turned around and stopped dead in her tracks. Reaching up, she tugged on the wires to her earbuds, so they came out of her ears. "Oh, hi, how long have you been standing there?" asked Acelyn with pink cheeks.

"Oh, just long enough to see you twitch your bottom like you do your tail," he said with a heart dropping smile.

"Oh," she said lowing her face and backing away.

Quickly stepping forward he reached out and grabbed her arm "Please do not go, I found your dancing very enchanting."

Looking up with wide eyes, "What? Why would you say that?"

"All I meant is that I like the way you dance. You must have been a gypsy in a past life."

"I don't think so; my foster mom is a Vegas show girl. I learned how to dance from her."

"So, what were you dancing to? I did not hear any music?" he asked.

With a small smile she walked over to him, "With this. The music comes out of these."

Looking down at the earbuds "I do not understand I still can't hear any music."

Smiling and shaking her head "Sometimes I forget that you are not from here." Leaning up on her tip toes she reached up and put the earbuds in his ears. Anton lifted his hands and laid them on her waist to help balance her, so she did not fall. Slowly she lowered back down to the floor, but Anton did not move his hands. She looked down at her iPod and hit play. She laughed when she saw Anton's reaction to his ears getting assaulted by Getting Your Sexy Back by Justin Timberlake.

Pulling the earbuds out of his ears he looked down and could not help but smile at the delight and laughter in Acelyn's eyes. "What is so funny?" asked Anton

"The. Look. On. Your. Face," she managed to say between bouts of laughter.

"What was wrong with my face?" asked Anton

"No, you silly dragon, the look you had when the music started," she giggled. "Your eyes got all big, your nose wrinkled, and your eyebrows flew up into your hair line. It was just funny and kind of cute," explained Acelyn.

"Show me."

"What?"

"Show me. Show me what it looked like."

Laughing she shook her head, "I can't."

Anton did not want to lose this easy mood with her, so he was trying anything to keep her from closing off from him. Pushing his bottom lip out in a pout "Pretty, pretty please try," Anton pouted.

Rolling her eyes, she tried to remake his face. She failed horribly but it sent them both into a fit of laughter causing her to lean her head on his chest. In that moment, Anton had the answer. He knew in his heart why she was his mate. But how was he going to get her to realize it so she would quit fighting their destiny.

Anton raised one hand and placed it under her chin and lifted her face so that he could gaze into her eyes.

"Pretty princess, can I ask you a question?"

"Um, I think you just did," she said with a shaky smile. "Yes, Anton you can ask."

"Why do you shy away from me?"

"I don't shy away from you. I just don't believe that someone's fate is written out before they were born."

"Oh, sweetheart, let me show you how different it can be." Before she could react, he closed the distance between them and captured her lips with his. Placing her hand firmly on Anton's chest with all intentions to push him away, she stopped all her movement when the weirdest feeling came over her. First the explosion of emotion that went off, a piercing pain stabbed her heart then a sunburst of warmth exploded within her. Now she was so confused she had never felt anything like this before. Instead of feeling awkward and out of place with Anton, she felt warm, safe, and loved. Startled by this feeling she pushed on his chest just so she could get some breathing room. Anton reluctantly released his hold on her and let her step back.

"Are you alright, my dove?

Nodding slowly, she cleared her throat so she could speak. "Anton, I don't know, I mean I just don't think this will work. I just don't think it is time to see if something between us will work," she explained with her cheeks turning pink.

"My dear Acelyn, you and I are fated, our souls are now one. Please do not be scared I will never hurt you. I will always put you first and make sure you are always safe," explained Anton softly so that he would not spook her anymore.

"Anton, see it is stuff like that, that makes me want to run. Also, what I feel for you scares me."

"What can I do to help you feel safer so you would want to stay?"

"Let me get to know you, I just need some time without feeling pressured or that I have no choice."

"Okay I will do anything you need me to do. What can I do right now?"

With a devilish grin, "Well Mr. Mysterious, you can help me cook dinner."

"I so do not know how to cook."

"Well, it is a good time to learn," she said with a smile.

Chapter Five

While the new-found family was having their victory dinner, Bella was cooking up a little something as well. In the potions room in the giant castle between realms Bella mixed a brew that might help her sneak out of the castle to help Mya and Ember. Looking down at the beautiful handheld gold mirror that was accented with silver filigree, she watched the images flicker then go black. Bella took a deep breath and turned her heartbreak in to rage and finished the potion she was working on. Looking down at her bubbling pot she tossed in a hand full of dried passionflower, valerian root, chamomile, then she drizzled in just a little bit of honey for taste. Then Bella chanted:

> *May these herbs be strong and true*
> *And make my love fall into a deep slumber*
> *Let the memories from when he was happy fill his heart*
> *So that the darkness will loosen its hold.*
> *May these herbs take hold and not let up until I return*
> *So, mote it be.*

As Bella chanted, the potion changed colors from a deep blood red to a soft pink then went clear. Once it had cooled, she put it in a small glass vial. Bella wandered the castle halls pondering on how she was going to get Kahn to drink the potion. Then a thought came to her suddenly. Bella took off like a bat out of hell to the kitchen. Just when she was putting the finishing touches to her plan she heard!

"Bella, where are you?"

"I am in the kitchen, my love," Bella answered back.

The heavy wood door slammed into the wall when Kahn entered.

"What are you doing? We have servants if you need something," Kahn spat.

"I know my love, but I wanted to do something nice for you. You know, to show you how happy I am, to be here with you," said Bella with a warm smile hoping he wouldn't see right through her plan.

Kahn's features and his body relaxed. "What do you have there?" Pointing at the tray she was picking up.

"That my dear is a surprise," she said while walking out the door with the tray. Looking back over her shoulder, "Come on if you want your surprise."

Bella turned around and walked through the door, swaying her hips just a little more than normal.

Kahn followed Bella to their sitting room in their bed chambers. "What are we doing in here, Bella?"

"Well, I figured this is one place in this castle that we would have some privacy. Now come sit down, I made your favorite."

"And what would that be?" asked Kahn with a small smile.

"I made you cheesy tomato soup, grilled cheese, and southern sweet tea."

Eager, he sat across from Bella and watched her dish up their food. "What kind of cheese did you use?"

With a bright smile she looked up at him, "Gouda, Provolone, and Munster, all your favorites. my love."

Once his plate was in front of him, he dug in. Knowing that eating the grilled cheese would make him thirsty, she poured him a glass of tea. Kahn picked up the tea and drank greedily. Once the glass was drained dry, he held the glass out to her, "May I have some more…please?" asked Kahn.

Bella picked up the pitcher and poured him another glass of tea, "Of course, you can have as much as you want. I made this lunch just for you," said Bella.

"Why does the tea taste different than I remember?" asked Kahn looking at his glass of tea.

"Well, I made it a little different this time, sometimes I like lemons, chamomile, and mint in my tea." Bella watched Kahn very closely hoping that he would not think too much about the chamomile in the tea. "Do you like it?"

Kahn took another drink "Yes, my dear, I do."

Letting out a breath that she did not even know that she was holding she reached over and laid her hand on his. "Good, I am glad you like it. I want to share many things that I have learned since we were apart."

They sat and talked while they finished eating, and Bella waited patiently for the signs that Khan was feeling the effects of the potion. It took almost an hour for Khan to fall asleep. Walking over to the love seat she took a wool blanket and covered Khan before leaving the castle.

Once Bella reached the outside of the castle, she took off running and shifted forms in mid stride. Being a liger made it easier for her to reach the edge of Kahn's royal estate faster. Once at the edge she closed her glowing ocean blue eyes and pawed the ground. The air started to shimmer in front of her and a portal opened to Aadya. Each step she took shook the ground that echoed through the realm. Stopping and looking around at the place that once was under her rule, she let out a bone-rattling roar and collapsed.

After a few minutes, she shook her head knowing that mourning the past was not helping the future. Getting back to her feet she took off running towards the Deadlands. Bella was hoping that she would find someone or a spirit that was not affected by the curse that could help, by telling her where the Goddesses Three could be found. Bella was so focused on what she was doing she never noticed the Black Phoenix that was following her in the sky. On the edge of the Deadlands, Malic dropped in front of Bella and spoke, "Hello Aunt Bella, my name is Malic."

Chapter Six

Bella skidded to a stop turning her head from side to side, she studied the black bird. Slowly she faded back to her human form then slowly asked, "Who did you say you were?"

Tipping his head in respect to her he replied, "My name is Malic."

Shaking her head, "That cannot be, my nephew's name was Malic, and he died when he was three."

"Yes, Aunt Bella, I remember when I died. But I was given a second chance at life so that I could help my sisters in their fight against Morgana."

"How is this possible?"

"Apollo came to me and asked if I were strong enough to help in this war, I told him that I would do anything to help my family. That includes freeing my Uncle Kahn, I know that if he were not poisoned with the darkness, he would have never hurt me."

Bella walked over to Malic and rested her hand on top of his head and gave his soft feathers a small stroke. Bringing her other hand up to cradle his head in her hands she bent down and softly kissed the tip of his beak. Standing back up and looking Malic in the eyes "Malic, my sweet, sweet boy, I have missed you every day. I love you very much, and you are right, your sisters and your uncle need our help. So, I must ask you for something. Where do I need to go to meet up with Mya, Ember, and Nightwing? I am going to help them set Luna, Star, and Night free from the stone."

"I will help you, Aunt Bella, but you must promise me something in return." You must not tell my sisters about me. When it is time, I will let them know who I am. I do not want them distracted from their current mission. Do I have your word?"

"Yes, you have my word, I will not tell them who you are. Only because I agree with you on not distracting them. Your sisters are amazing. They have big and kind hearts, and because of the type of people they are, that is exactly what they would do. They would add you to the list of people to save."

"Okay, you can find Mya, Ember, and Nightwing on the edge of the Enchanted Forest. They are headed to the castle. In the courtyard you will find Luna, Star, Night, and my mother and father."

"Malic sweetheart, your parents are dead."

"No, Aunt Bella they are still alive. Just like the rest of this realm they were cursed to stone. They turned before Uncle Khan could kill them."

"Then I will free them as well." Turning so she could shift, Malic stopped her.

"No, it is not up to you to free them. Once my sisters win this war, they will be freed just like the rest of Aadya. If we tamper with too many things it could shift the balance and my sisters could lose. Plus, we do not want Morgana to figure out we are helping the girls."

Bella lowered her head "Malic, she is my sister, I just cannot let her stay like that."

Bella felt a change in the air, the temperature dropped leaving a chill. Lifting her head, she looked at Malic and instantly took a step back. His big black eyes had turned crimson. He puffed out his chest and black and blue flames danced on the edge of his feathers. Leaning forward he towered over Bella, he spoke in a deep booming voice. "Do you think they mean nothing to me; they are my parents. You act like they were only taken from you. I was three when they were taken away from me, my sisters were only two days old when they were sent away. So, I do not want to hear that you are going to defy me. You will do only what you are meant to do or so help me and the gods I will stop you. Are we clear, Aunt Bella?"

All Bella could do is nod her head yes. Knowing what he was saying was true. She was being selfish and not putting the realm first. "Malic, I am sorry. I will not interfere. I will stay with the plan."

Malic instantly calmed down, leaning forward he rubbed the side of his face on her cheek to wipe away the tears that fell. "I do not tell you this because I am being mean. We must stick to the plan so that my sisters are safe. Also, if we change anything in the plan that has been laid out, my sisters could not only lose the war but also lose their lives. So please, I beg of you, follow the plan."

Reaching up to stroke Malic's neck, "I promise you; I will follow the plan. Now I must go if I am going to make it in time to help Mya, Ember, and Nightwing." Rising to her tiptoes she kissed the side of his head then her form faded. Nodding her head and pawing the ground she said farewell one more time and took off.

Chapter Seven

As Bella ran, she looked at the world that was once her home years ago. Her heart hurt to see her homeland in shambles. The once vibrant and full of life world was now dull, gray, and lifeless. Just on the edge of the estate that was once her castle she stopped at the tree that Kahn carved their names in and took a minute to remember. The big oak always had a family of birds that lived in it, she loved to come and sit under the tree with Kahn and listen to the birds chirp and sing. Now it just looked dead, no birds singing, no rustling leaves in the wind. Standing up on her hind legs, she placed a paw in the center of the heart that held their names. Saying a silent vow that she would help fix the realm, and Kahn, she lowered back to the ground and proceeded to the castle.

Upon approaching the castle, Bella slowed her movements to almost a crawl. When she reached the front door to the castle she stilled, trying to decide if she wanted to enter. Just when she was about to cross the threshold of the castle doors she heard, "Come on Ember, there is no time to waste, Queen Bella must be here already."

Looking up and trying to figure out where the sound came from, her ears and tail twitched.

"What do you mean? Queen Bella disappeared years ago," asked Nightwing.

"Luna, Star, and Night helped Queen Bella escape and return to Edan, so that she would be able to survive to help the girls save our realm," explained Mya.

Hearing Mya's voice, Bella took off running towards them. When she got close enough, Ember was the first to see her and let out a scream and hid behind one of Nightwing's legs. Wanting to protect his tiny friend he lowered his head and let out a volley of flames at Bella. Shifting in mid run she lifted her hand and deflected the flames. Bella walked with her head held high, proud, and strong like a queen should be. Walking up to Mya she enfolded her friend into a warm hug.

"It is good to see you again, my friend," said Bella with a warm smile.

"Yes, and it is good to see you still in one piece," Mya scolded. "How could you not follow the plan we had? It has been a tough task to keep your nieces on the right track. They think they need to rescue you."

"I am fine, and I do not need them to rescue me. I will be fine. I am doing what I needed to help them in the upcoming war. I came here to help you three free Luna, Star, and Night. Then I must get back to Kahn's castle before he wakes. So, we do not have time to stand here and argue what I should have done. Now get moving, and that is an order from your queen," commanded Bella pointing at the castle.

The group bowed to Queen Bella, she nodded in acknowledgment then her form faded, and she took off toward the castle. With the others following close behind her, they entered the cold lifeless castle that once was full of color and life. The entrance to the great hall was once full of warm colors that was accented in gold and rich warm browns, and marble floors that were black, red, and trimmed in silver was now gray with no feeling of life.

Bella transformed and walked up to the throne room doors and gave them a push. No matter how hard she pushed, they would not budge. The others walked up to help Bella. Nightwing lowered his head and placed it firmly on the door. Mya and Ember also placed their hands on the doors. Looking over at her friends, Bella counted "1, 2, 3, push," Bella bellowed. The stone cracked and crumbled away from the doors, with both hands Bella pushed on the doors and they swung open. Bella just stared at the sight in front of her.

The room looked untouched. The marble floor looked like it had just been polished, the gold shined and the pictures of her, Anastasia, Alexzander, and Kahn looked as if they were just painted. Then her eyes settled on the thrones, all four still sat there. She walked up to hers and ran her hand over the warm mahogany wood. Reaching a shaky hand down to feel the red crushed velvet, a tear fell for her sister. Quickly wiping it away knowing there was nothing she could do for Anastasia.

Bella stood and turned around to the others, "Come, let us go, we are running out of time." Shifting back to her liger form, she took off through the castle to the courtyard. Flying up to Bella, Mya asked, "How did the throne room go untouched by the curse?"

Stopping and shifting, Bella looked at Mya, "Because I was in Edan. When Kahn cast the curse, his heart was bleeding from the loss of me being gone. He wanted one thing that was mine untouched," Bella explained.

Once they reached the courtyard, Bella ran to where her sister stood in stone. Remembering what Malic had said she turned away from her sister and went to the Goddesses Three. All Bella could do was stand there and stare at the three beauties who were incased in stone. They were frozen in time. Luna with her hair blowing in the wind, her head tipped up and arms extended up reaching to the Gods for help. Bella could tell just by the way Star was frozen she was trying to put a shield around the king and queen. Star's head was looking down with one hand in a pouch and the other arm stretched out in front of her. Night looked like she was gazing into your soul, arms stretched out in front of her cupping an orb in the palms of her hands.

"Oh my, even cursed they are still beautiful," whispered Ember.

"Do you think they were trying to help the king and queen when the curse took hold?" asked Nightwing.

"Yes, they were here when Kahn attacked. They had just sent the princesses to Edan. But it looks like they were unable to escape the curse. Okay, let us get them out of that stone. Mya and Ember, we will say a spell while Nightwing uses his flames," said Bella.

Chapter Eight

They all gathered around the Goddesses raising their hands to the sky they chanted:

Hail to the gods hear our plea,
Help us free the Goddesses Three,
Help guide Nightwing's flame to strike good and true,
Hail to the gods hear our plea,
So, mote it be.

Lightning cracked and the sky went black. As the flames hit their mark the wind started to howl, and the clouds parted. Bella and the others looked to the sky and fell to their knees to pay respect to the god that had answered their plea. Zeus stood on a cloud looking down, and his blond hair seemed to glow, his all-white eyes had sparks in them. Arching back his arm he threw a lightning bolt down and hit the stone that incased the Goddesses. Bending his knees, he jumped and landed in front of Bella, unaware that the others had backed away to give her some space. Bella observed the God that towered over her. Every muscle was finely chiseled now that she was closer, she noticed that it looked like his hair was made from the sun itself. His eyes did not have sparks; it was electricity that was in them. He stood at least 4 feet taller than Bella, he was wearing a white cloth that was tied at one shoulder and draped across his chest down to his hip, the bottom of the cloth was just below his knees. He was wearing sandals that had leather straps that crisscrossed up his calves. He spoke in a deep booming voice, "Queen Bella, you have done a great service to me by freeing my daughters. You may have one wish and one wish only."

With her heart torn in half knowing that she could only pick one. She looked back at her sister and swore to find another way to save her. Bowing her head, she asked the only thing that felt right in her heart. "All mighty Zeus, would you please tell me how to take the darkness out of Kahn's heart?"

"Yes, it can be done but it will not be easy. You will need the blood of a dragon pixie and from the three princesses. You will need the nectar from the rare fire orchid, and my daughters will be able to help with the rest. Now you will need to have Khan here while Luna, Star, and Night perform the ritual. Be safe Queen Bella, and may you have the speed and strength of the gods." Without saying anything else he turned away from the others, walked over to his daughters and kissed each one on the forehead, and disappeared.

Luna, Star, and Night walked over to their rescuers and bowed. Luna was the first to speak, "Your Majesty, thank you for freeing us. I will gladly fulfill your request."

"Queen Bella, I am glad you are healthy and safe," said Star.

"You are just as beautiful as the day we helped you get to Edan," commented Night.

"No, I have gotten much older, but you three are just the same" said Bella.

"Queen Bella, we do not age we are immortal, but our hearts have aged. The whole time we were imprisoned we were awake, and we could hear the realm cry for help. We could feel its pain, feel it die. The princesses need to come home and set Aadya free," said Luna.

"The girls are trying, they are working on a way to free their sister now," said Mya.

Luna flew into a rage, her beautiful blue eyes turned white, and a storm passed through them. What do you mean save their sister?" asked Luna.

"Well, Kahn got to her before the girls could find each other," Mya explained.

Once again, the sky turned black as night. Luna, Star, and Night floated three feet off the ground then they spoke in unison, "Where was her guardian? He was assigned to take her to her sisters and get her back here safely."

Taking a few steps back, Bella joined the others looking over at Nightwing. Mya and Ember were tucked safely under his wings. Standing tall Bella met

36

the Goddesses head on. "When the portal was open for them to leave here, Coda was put in the Shadow realm, and Zanderley was attacked by Kahn. Jaz was with her until Kahn knocked him out and took the Princess. They have found her, and they are going to go and rescue her," said Bella.

"If the balance is messed up, they could lose this war, and Aadya would be lost forever. The Fates must be rescued, we must know what they see," Luna said.

Luna looked at Bella. "You need to get back to the castle before Kahn wakes. Mya, I need you to get the flower we need to cure Kahn." Nodding Mya flew off toward the Firelands. "Nightwing, Ember, go and find Kane and Catarina and help them with the Fates." Nodding they took flight and headed into the woods.

"Thank you for helping me," said Bella then her form faded. She pawed the ground and went through the portal.

After the portal closed, Star looked at her sisters and said, "Queen Bella has changed."

"How so, sister?" asked Night

"Queen Bella is stronger than she was when she came to us for help all those years ago," Luna answered.

"Well, let us go and see what we can do to help the princesses," said Luna before grabbing her sisters' hands and walking over to Queen Anastasia and King Alexzander.

"For all the hard work the Princesses have done and will do let us free their parents," said Luna.

The Goddesses surrounded the king and queen and reached for the heavens.

All Hail Zeus hear our plea
Help us free Queen Anastasia and King Alexzander
So that they may live to see another day
So, mote it be.

Lightning touched their fingertips; they lowered their arms pulling the lightning down from the sky and aimed it at the stone. The stone popped and cracked then crumbled away.

Queen Anastasia fell to her knees then crawled to her beloved Alexzander. "Hold on my love, and I will try and stop the bleeding," reaching with her hands and placing them on his chest. Luna crouched down and laid her hand on Anastasia's shoulder. "Let us help my queen." Star and Night joined their sister laying their hands on the queen and king. The next thing Anastasia knew she was in a place that was filled with flowers and bright white columns. Looking up she was met with the all-white eyes of Zeus. He looked at Luna, Star, and Night then spoke, "My daughters, take them to the palace."

Once in the palace they were met my Hera. She was holding onto a gold goblet. Placing the cup to Alexzander's lips she spoke softly, "Drink, brave king." When Alexzander drank, Anastasia watched his wounds close and heal with no trace. Looking up at Hera with tears in her eyes, "Thank you, mother goddess," said Anastasia while holding on to Alexzander.

"You need to drink too, brave queen." Hera nodded at Anastasia while lifting the goblet to her lips. After drinking, she looked down at herself and Alexzander, a gasp left her lips and her heart started to race. They were dressed in all white, Alexander was dressed in a white tunic and leather sandals. Anastasia was dressed in a white gown and leather sandals. Looking up at Hera, "I do not understand, why we are dressed like this?" asked Anastasia.

"We have given you and Alexzander the nectar of the gods, you are no longer mortal. You have been given the gift of immortality, you are now Demi Gods," said Hera with a smile.

Chapter Nine

After dinner was cleaned up, they all worked together to pick up the yard so there was no trace of the fight earlier that day. As the hero's finished up, a storm raged outside. Anton watched Acelyn as she watched the storm. Now that they were linked, he could feel how uneasy she was about the storm. Walking over to Acelyn he rubbed his hands up and down her arm trying to pass on his calming nature. After about five minutes, she relaxed into Anton's embrace.

Temprance smiled to herself enjoying seeing her sister calm and happy. Hating to interrupt the peace that her sister had found she spoke, "I know there is a bad ass storm blowing out there, but we still need to go rescue our other sister."

Pulling out of Anton's embrace, Acelyn looked at the group and said, "I agree we need to figure out what we are going to do." Reaching out to grab Anton's hand she pulled him into the living room and over to the couch. Once he was seated, she curled up next to him hoping it would have the same effect as by the window.

Feeling her unease come back, he lifted his arm so she could snuggle in closer. Once she was settled, he wrapped his arm around her once again. When everyone was seated Temprance called the meeting to order.

"Okay, so have we figured out how we are going to get to Greece?"

Jewel stood up and went to the center of the room, "Yes, I am going to take you." It was so quiet you could hear a pin drop.

Sitting up; Acelyn asked, "How are you going to get all of us to Greece?"

With a big smile, "With my new powers." Then Jewel closed her eyes, the air shimmered and made little popping sounds, next to her a portal opened. "Like this, I can open up portals, I can take us anywhere."

Moving closer to the portal, Temprance and Acelyn looked at a place on the other side. "Umm Jewel, where is that at?" asked Temprance.

Jewel looked at the portal, "That is Aadya just on the edge of the royal estate." Looking down at the girls Jewel explained, "That is your castle, princesses."

Jumping back like they got shocked, the girls shook their heads, "That is what we are fighting to save," said Temprance.

"It looks lifeless, what is there to save?" asked Acelyn.

Getting up to join the girls, Zeke and Anton stood behind them. "No, the place you are fighting to save was once vibrant and full of life. Do not give up hope because of what it looks like now. Try and think what it will look like when you save it," said Anton.

"How are we going to picture what it would look like if we have never seen it? If we go by the picture through the portal it is dull, and gray, and lifeless," said Acelyn.

"Hold on a second," said Anton, then looked at Zeke.

Temprance looked back at the guys, "You know I hate it when you guys do that crap."

"Do what, Tempie?" asked Acelyn.

"Them doing that mind talking crap. If they have something to say they need to share it with the class, and not keep it between them."

"Hey, I agree," said Acelyn elbowing Anton in the stomach.

"Oomph, Why the hell did you hit me?"

"For keeping secrets from me," said Acelyn crossing her arms.

"I am sorry my Dove, it is just so easy when we have been doing it for years. I will make you a promise that I will always try and include you from now on," said Anton leaning down and kissing the top of her head.

"So, what were you talking about then?" asked the girls in unison.

"We were talking about using one of our powers we have not used in an awfully long time. With your permission we are going to show you our memories."

Acelyn looked back over her shoulder and asked, "You can do that?"

"Yes, with your permission and a lot of concentration."

Acelyn and Temprance got all excited and danced in place. "Well let's do it," they said.

"Okay the first thing we need you to do is kneel and face us." Sinking to their knees the guys followed suit. Placing their hands on the girl's shoulders, "Now grab your sister's hand, close your eyes, breathe out, relax, and open your mind," said Anton.

Temprance and Acelyn did what was asked of them. Everything went quiet and an image started to form. The castle stood tall and full of life. There were people and creatures roaming the grounds. Roses all different colors were in full bloom filled the courtyard. There were two ladies and two men chasing each other while the sun glinted off their crowns. The more they observed, Temprance and Acelyn realized that two of the people were their parents, and the other two were their Aunt Bella and Uncle Kahn. The trees swayed and rustled in the wind; the prettiest sound came from the birds singing. The colors were so vibrant, the grass and leaves in the trees were the richest color of green they had ever seen.

They looked up to the mountains to see the dragons flying around. Some were doing their mating ritual, it looked like a dance in the sky. They were doing loops and swoops one even flew upside down for a second. The smell of a campfire caught the girl's attention, so they looked over to the right and saw fauns dancing around a fire and one was playing a wooden flute. The woods were full of fairy lights and beautiful songs were sung by wood nymphs.

Next thing they felt was like they were flying. Looking down they saw a place that looked like a graveyard. They landed in a huge field of flowers of all colors and types. There were red poppies, yellow daffodils, white daisies, and purple irises. There were little bunnies eating thistles and baby deer were playing as well. Taking back off they flew over a part of the land that was full of different kinds of flowers and red dragons. Multicolored phoenixes tended their nests. A huge volcano sat in the center of this place and around its base was a lake of lava.

A roaring sound came from the east. Flying over there the sight almost blinded them. The sun hitting the ocean was breath taking. When the sun hit the water, it looked like the water was filled with emeralds. There were blue sea dragons playing in the water and tending to their young. Looking upon the rock there were mermaids sunbathing, their tails were gorgeous. Their scales looked like they were made from sapphires, rubies, and diamonds.

As the sun started to set, they seem to fly higher and looking down at the sight took their breath away. The land around the castle twinkled with little lights. Looking over to the forest where they had seen the campfire, they could see lights in little holes in the trees where the fairies lived. Looking around taking one last look everything went black.

Opening their eyes slowly they looked up at Anton and Zeke with tears in their eyes. Acelyn wrapped her arms around Anton and just cried. "Shh, my Dove, we will help our home. We will heal the land once more."

Chapter Ten

Unable to sleep, Acelyn wandered in the dark house while everyone else was sleeping. The storm still raged on and every time the thunder boomed, or lightning cracked Acelyn would jump. Deciding a cup of tea might calm her nerves, she went into the kitchen to put the kettle on. Acelyn did not spook easily but something about this storm had her on edge. She has had this uneasy feeling from the beginning of the storm.

Unable to sleep Anton tossed and turned in the bed. Knowing that his sleepless night was coming from Acelyn, he decided to go and check on her. Heading down the hallway to her room he found it empty. Being a dragon has its advantages, sonic hearing being one of them, so closing his eyes he listened to the noises in the house. Even in the dead of night Anton picked up on many sounds, the creaking of the settling house, wind blowing outside, but over all of that he heard Acelyn's tea kettle about to whistle on the stove.

Anton just watched Acelyn study the storm, speaking softly so that he would not spook her any more than she was. "If you are scared of storms why are you watching it through the biggest window in the house?"

Turning to look at him she answered, "I am not scared of storms, there is just something about this storm that doesn't seem right." Then she turned and looked back out the sliding glass doors. Walking over to Acelyn, Anton walked up behind her and wrapped his arms around her waist and pulled her back, so she was snuggled up against his chest. He instantly felt her nerves calm.

They stood there in silence only the sounds of the storm sounded. When the kettle sounded Acelyn jumped, leaning down he kissed her temple. "Stay here my Dove, I will get you a cup of tea." As soon as Anton left, she felt the loss of him. Acelyn once again felt uneasy, anxious, and lonely. Once Anton had returned, he handed her the tea and pulled her back, so she was in the same position before he left.

What seemed like hours they just stood there in complete harmony; Anton held her while she drank her tea. Keeping an eye on the storm that had her uneasy Anton searched the shadows just to make sure there was no one lurking there. Leaning down so he could speak softly in Acelyn's ear, "What makes you so uneasy about this storm?" Acelyn let out an involuntary shudder before she spoke, "I am not sure but there is just something about it that doesn't seem right, watch the lightning."

"What about it?" he asked.

"I have seen bright lightning before, but I have never seen lightning so bright that when it strikes it makes it almost daylight outside. It makes the shadows so much darker; you would never know if something was lurking. Plus, ever since the fight earlier I have felt that someone was watching us. I have no proof; it is just a feeling."

"Well, you have all of us here to help if something was out there, you are no longer alone Princess, you have a family. I know we said we would not talk about us, but I just wanted to let you know that I will never let anything bad happen to you. We have a big day tomorrow and, on that note, you need to try and get some sleep. Come on I will walk you to your room," said Anton. Releasing her from his warm embrace he reached and clasped her hand in his and pulled her over to the sink to put her cup away.

Walking up the stairs Acelyn was dreading on going into her cold, lonely room alone. Trying to think of a way to keep Anton close to her without letting him know she was enjoying his presence. "Umm. Hey Anton, does it hurt going through a portal?"

"No, what would make you think it would hurt?"

Shrugging her shoulders, "I don't know," she said turning away from him.

Walking over to Acelyn and gripping her shoulders, he turned her around and looked into her beautiful green eyes. Once he turned her around, she lowered her head using her hair to make a curtain to hide her face. Gently he lifted her face and with the other hand he pushed her long raven locks over her shoulders. He saw many emotions pass through her eyes, excitement, fear, trepidation, then finally calm. He made a vow that she would be the one to make the next move. Keeping his word, he leaned down and kissed her on the forehead. Moving his hand to cradle the back of her head he slowly moved her head to rest on his chest.

Acelyn wrapped her arms around his waist and finally found her tranquility she had looked for this all her life. Acelyn had always felt she was out of step with everyone around her. Focusing on Anton's heartbeat, she noticed it was in sync with hers. Lifting her head, she looked at Anton and said, "Your heartbeat matches mine, how is that possible?"

"Because my Dove, our souls are now one. I know this scares you, but you are my mate."

"What happens if you decide that one day you no longer want me? Then I will be crushed because of what I feel for you."

When Anton looked deep into her eyes, he knew she was speaking the truth. He also knew he needed to tell her the truth even if it frightened her. "Acelyn, I need to tell you things and some of them may scare you, are you willing to listen to me?" Making a gulping sound she nodded yes.

"First off, you will never have to worry that I will get tired of you or fall out of love with you. I am a dragon, and we mate for life; I knew from the moment when I kissed you the first time that you would be my queen and be the mother of my children. You and your sisters are incredibly special, not only are you going to be Queens of Aadya, but you can bare dragon born children. As your mate and king, I will live out the rest of my days as a human." Noticing she was not breathing he stroked a thumb across her cheek. "Dove, breath," Anton spoke softly.

Acelyn let out the breath she was holding and looked up at Anton with wonder and fear. "So, we are fated?" she asked.

"Yes, my Dove, but do not look at it as a curse. You have found someone to stand by you no matter what happens. I love you Acelyn, and I will love you until my last breath. Is that something you can live with?" asked Anton.

"I think that is something I can live with. I just need time to get used to someone being there for me and loving me as much as I love them."

"Why Princess, did you just admit that you love me?"

With cheeks turning pink she rose to her tip toes and kissed him. Once she lowered back to the floor, she gave him a shy smile, "Maybe."

Filled with joy he picked her up by the waist and spun her around in a circle then tossed her on the bed. Crawling over her smiling he cradled her face in his hands and kissed her soft and gentle. Placing a hand firmly on his chest she stopped him from coming any closer. "Just because I was able to tell you how I feel does not mean I am ready to have sex with you."

"Acelyn my Dove, I have waited five hundred years for you I do not mind waiting longer. We will go at your pace." Leaning down he placed one more kiss on her soft pink lips then shifted so he was lying beside her.

"Will you stay in here with me tonight and hold me while I sleep?" she asked it so quietly Anton almost never heard the question.

"Yes, I will stay. Now close your eyes and get some rest, sweet princess of mine."

Without another word she closed her eyes and drifted off to sleep. Anton stayed awake to keep watch; he did not want to alarm the sleeping beauty lying next to him, but he did see something moving in the shadows earlier. She was also correct in saying that this storm was not natural, she was still new to her powers so she could not feel the magic in the air. But he could feel it, and it felt wicked.

As he held Acelyn while she slept, he watched the storm rage on. Looking at his surroundings he felt that this room was not fit for his queen. He started to dream and plan on how he would shower her in silks, jewels, flowers, and anything else she wanted, his mate would want for nothing. Just as he was about to fall asleep, he noticed the black raven sitting on the window ledge watching them.

Chapter Eleven

In her hut deep in the Desiccated Woods, Morgana flew into a fit of rage. The madder she got the harder the storm raged on in Edan. She sent a raven to spy on the so-called heroes so that she could form a new plan. She knew that she was running out of time, because if they got to their sister their bond would be unbreakable. Maybe if she could get to the third sister, she could turn her against the others. Then after the sisters killed each other then she would kill the last one standing and end the royal blood line that way.

But the first thing on her list was to go back to the underworld and get another hell hound to replace her dear Orthrus. This time she would make sure it was meaner and more deadly. Working quickly, she gathered what she would need to head to the underworld. Morgana stepped out of her hut into the swamp, she turned and looked at her hut, with a wave of a hand she made it disappear. Now that her hideout was cloaked, she set out for the underworld.

Looking around her woods she sneered at the memory of what it looked like. The Desiccated Woods was once home to the dragon pixies and woodland dragons. The woods were called The Dreaming Woods and filled with life. It was destroyed long before the curse took over Aadya. Morgana smiled to herself remembering how she hunted and drained every pixie dragon until they were no more. With a snarl she remembered about Jewel, not only was there still a pixie dragon still alive but one of royal blood. She mentally put that on the checklist, but she needed to stay focused on the task at hand.

After walking for a mile Morgana looked around for a spot where the veil between worlds was thin, reaching in her pouch she grabbed a fist full of ashes from a phoenix and tossed it in front of her. There was a popping sound and the world just seemed to split open, once she stepped through, she noticed this was going to be harder than last time. Walking to the opening in the rock wall she noticed she was on the edge of the river Styx.

Morgana debated how she was going to get to the other side without Hades guards or Charon seeing her. If Hades ever found out that she had snuck into the underworld he would make sure she would never leave. Knowing she could not swim across because of the lost souls that would drag her down to the bottom, she decided she would have to take her chances and cross the bridge. Morgana pulled the shawl she was wearing up to cover her head and face. Cursing Hades for having a magic barrier in the underworld so using magic to disguise herself was out of the question.

When Morgana was confident that she had hidden her appearance enough she started to weave herself through the souls waiting for Charon to take them to Elysian Fields. When Morgana was almost at the bridge, she felt the tip of a spear poke her in the back, "You there stop! You may not cross the bridge; you must wait here for the boat."

Turning, keeping her eyes cast down she spoke in a shaky voice, "I am headed to the palace to plead to Hades to gain entrance to Paradise. You see I have no family so when I died there was no one to give me a coin for passage. That is why I must plead my case. Please help a lonely old soul."

The guards nodded. "You may pass, do not stray, go straight to the palace because if you are found where you are not allowed you will find yourself forever in Tartarus instead of Paradise." Nodding in acknowledgement, she quickly left the guards and crossed the bridge. Once across the bridge the next challenge awaited her. Now she had to cross the Plain of Judgment to get past the guards at the entrance of Tartarus. While crossing the Plain of Judgment she reminded herself that she needed to keep her plans out of her head. Even with her still being alive she could still be judged and sent to Tartarus for all eternity. Just on the edge of Plain of Judgment she could see Hades palace. She gave the same story to the guards at the entrance of Tartarus and they also let her pass with the same warning.

Walking up the palace walk she could feel the eyes of the guards and the tormented souls following her. Morgana knew that she would have to take her next steps very carefully if she did not want to end up in Tartarus. Morgana waited for just the right moment for the guards to look the other way so she could slip into the shadows. Very quietly Morgana made her way around the palace by sticking to the shadows. Once she got close enough, she could hear the Cerberus pups fighting. While keeping an eye out for guards she reached in her pouch and pulled out the bait she had prepared with the sleeping potion. Morgana hid in the shadows and waited for one of the pups. As one got closer, she could toss the bait where it would be noticed.

The only pup that came close enough was the runt of the litter. When he was in range, she tossed out the bait, the pup wandered over and started to eat the meat. Shortly after eating he fell asleep and Morgana grabbed his massive paw and pulled him all the way into the shadows. Quickly she reached into her pouch for the ashes and tossed them to put a rip in the veil. She then crossed over while taking her prize with her. Back in the Desiccated Woods she looked down at the pup, "Well I guess you will have to do." Morgana bent down and stroked the pup's left head. Reaching down she picked up a petrified vine and sprinkled some dust onto it.

The vine turned into a silver collar with fire rubies that matched the flames in his eyes, embellished on it. Leaning down she fastened the collar around his neck and said, "Your new name is Spike. You will answer to me and only me. May this collar be a reminder, that you are mine." Spike opened his eyes and started to snarl and back away from Morgana. "Spike, come here and sit," Morgana commanded. The pup instantly started to fight Morgana's command. The more he disobeyed, his collar glowed and gave the pup pain. "Spike, I said come here." The pup slowly walked to her, "Now sit." Once Spike sat the pain eased and went away. Reaching down Morgana patted him on his heads. "Now that was a good boy, come we have a lot of work to do." Morgana turned and walked back to where her hut was hidden with Spike by her side.

Chapter Twelve

Early the next morning Acelyn woke up wrapped around Anton like a vine. Her head was on his chest with her arm draped across his stomach and her leg was weaved in between his. She lay there quietly so she did not wake him. Acelyn was really starting to enjoy and depend on the safety she felt in his arms. The arm around her waist flexed and pulled her closer. Acelyn held her breath so she would not make any noise, she wanted him to think she was still sleeping.

After a few minutes she tried to steal a peek to see if he was awake. She cracked one eye open and met a pair of orange and red eyes. Hoping that she was not caught she closed it and snuggled back in. Anton knew Acelyn was awake, he knew as soon as her breathing changed. He had been awake for an hour before Acelyn was. Moving his hand up from her hip he slid his hand under the hem of her night shirt and rested his hand on her side. When she still did not move or say anything is when he launched his attack. Gripping her firmly he started to tickle until she was breathless and begged him to stop.

After squirming out of Anton's steel grasp, Acelyn quickly tied her hair into a messy bun, then she turned and launched herself at Anton. Acelyn straddled Anton pinning his arms under her knees. Placing her hands on his bare chest, she reveled in the feel of his chiseled body. Leaning forward she slid her hand up to his shoulders and placed a soft kiss on his lips. Bending her head down to the hollow of his neck she took in a deep breath, letting it out slowly she spoke softly, "I always love the way you smell." With a cocky grin, he asked, "And how do I smell?"

"Well, it depends, sometimes you smell like the ocean's breeze and other times you smell like a campfire."

"And why do you like it?"

Sitting back up so she was looking at him, "I love the smell of the ocean air because it is calming, the campfire makes me think of what it would be like curled up in front of a fire with my love."

Sliding his right hand out from under her knee he reached up and stroked her cheek, "I promise you, Dove, when this is all over, I will take you to the ocean and we will curl up in front of a campfire. We will watch the sun set over the ocean then I will make love to you under the stars." Reaching up he pulled her hair tie out letting her curls tumble down past her waist. Smiling Anton looked into her eyes and said, "I always love the look of you when your hair is wild and free of its bindings."

Sliding his hand to just above her ear while weaving his fingers in her hair, he gripped softly while guiding her face down to him. Anton kissed her softly letting her know that he was not going to rush her. Acelyn pulled back breathless, for the first time in her life she felt desire. Worried he went a step too far he pulled his left hand out from under her other knee and sat it on her waist. Bringing his other hand up to match the first, he massaged small circles with his thumbs hoping it would calm her nerves. "Are you okay?" asked Anton.

Sucking her bottom lip in to her mouth she nodded yes. Reaching down and gripping the hem of her shirt she lifted it over her head. Anton's eyes went wide, he sucked in a breath. Letting it out slowly he spoke "Acelyn, you have the body of a goddess."

Not knowing if it was from desire, or from what Anton said, her whole body blushed the color of a light pink rose. Not wanting him to say anything else she grabbed fists full of Anton's hair and met his lips with a fevered pitch. Wrapping one arm around her waist and bringing the other up to cradle her head, he rolled her beneath him. Anton moved from her lips to her neck where he left a tiny nip. Then he started moving down her bare chest stopping on her stomach.

Letting go of his hair, she gripped his strong shoulders, slowly losing her grip her hands slid off and landed on the bed. Feeling like the world was spinning all she could do was grip the sheets. Planting soft kisses on her stomach caused Acelyn to arch her back in ecstasy, so he waited for her body to relax. When she was still once more, he continued his assault of kisses. Acelyn watched him worship her body, he made her feel like a queen. With soft strokes he worked his hands down her body to the waist band of her sleep pants, stopping and waiting to see if it was okay to move forward. Biting her bottom lip Acelyn nodded slowly, lifting her lower half so Anton could remove them.

This was the part Acelyn was worried about once he was told it was okay. She was afraid that he would be fast and rough forgetting about her. Anton could sense that something was wrong not only by the look on her face but her whole body stiffened. Tossing the discarded sleep pants on the floor he stood up and removed his, when he returned to the bed, he laid next her. Acelyn's heart was racing, it felt like it was going to pound out of her chest. Anton turned Acelyn's head to place a kiss just below her ear and asked, "What is wrong Dove, why are you scared?"

"A couple of reasons I guess," she said with a slight shrug of her shoulders.

Leaning up on his elbow he noticed not only was her face turned away her eyes were shut. Gently gripping her chin with one hand he turned her face towards him "Dove, look at me please," Anton pleaded.

When she looked into his beautiful eyes, he noticed that Acelyn had a sheen of tears in hers.

"We need to be open and honest with each other. No matter what you have to say it will not make me mad or push me away. So, talk to me please, if we are moving too fast let me know and we can stop here, okay?"

Nodding she raised her hand and softly touched his cheek causing Anton to lean into it. "I am scared because I have never done this before. I am worried you will be rough, and it will really hurt. Also, I am still a little scared once I give myself to you, you will not want me anymore," explained Acelyn.

"I will take care of you; I cannot promise that there will not be some pain. I would never hurt you on purpose, do not worry about this being your first time. This will also be my first time, remember dragons mate for life. Yes, I will still want you, I will worship the ground you walk on, you are my mate, the future mother of my children, my future wife, and you are my queen. You are a brave and beautiful person; I am the one that is lucky to have you as a mate. You have the bravery of a warrior, the heart of a saint, and the body of a goddess." Leaning down he placed a soft kiss on her lips, "Please, let me worship you." Looking down at Acelyn he noticed that a tear escaped and was sliding down her cheek, he leaned down so he could whisper in her ear, "I love you, Acelyn Queen of Aadya" then he kissed the tear away.

Like magic all her fears faded away and she sprang into action. The soft kisses and touches were a thing in the past, her back arched off the bed when he cupped her, causing her to crash over the peak for the first time. Collapsing back on the bed, Acelyn felt like all the bones in her body were gone. She felt the bed shift and Anton settle between her legs. Leaning down so that he was face to face with Acelyn he cradled her head in his hand. Anton spoke sweet and soothing things to Acelyn while he made sweet slow love to her.

After they both felt boneless and spent, Anton moved to lay beside Acelyn. With one arm he pulled her in close, so they were back in the position they were in when they woke. All that could be heard was their breathing. Out of the silence Acelyn spoke up, "I love you, my King."

Chapter Thirteen

The newfound lovers joined the others out under the pergola for breakfast. It did not go unnoticed that they were holding hands. Temprance just looked at her sister and smiled, knowing her sister's heart was now full of love like her own. Zeke looked over at Temprance wondering what made her heart flutter, then he noticed her looking at the new arrivals. Zeke looked at Anton and knew the reason for Temprance's reaction, Anton had found his mate.

Feeling like everyone was staring at her she asked, "Hey, Tempie, where did we get the new table?"

"Jewel fixed the old one with magic, she is really getting a handle on her new powers. I think her plan to portal jump will work. So, I would sit and eat, then we all need to go get supplies that we will need for the trip and get going. Zanderley has been Kahn's prisoner long enough, let us go get our sister."

Finding their seats, they ate breakfast and talked about their plan. Jaz kept thinking about the wonderful night that he had with Jewel. He felt their souls bond and he could tell she felt it too. He felt it all to be a dream. He never thought he would ever be a king, but Jewel asked him to rule next to her and the others. She was so beautiful, and he loved her so much already. Jaz knew he would protect her with his own life's blood. Jewel felt her heart go a flutter, so she looked down at Jaz and her own heart raced. All she could do is smile and quickly look away. Remembering just a few weeks ago she was alone, now she has a family and found her mate. Shaking her head, she wanted to get back on track, remembering what Draco told her years ago, "Remember little one a clouded or busy mind will get someone killed. There will be time for fun, love, and daydreaming after your work is done."

Since this would be the last meal in this house, they all worked together to clean it to where there would not be a trace that they were there. The guys grabbed the bags while the girls were in the kitchen packing one of Bella's enchanted bags with food and drinks. Anton peeked into the kitchen, only to meet Acelyn's smile and twinkling eyes as she put a couple of bottles of wine in the bag. Letting out a chuckle he winked at her and went to find Zeke.

Anton, Zeke, Coda, and Jaz were sitting in the living room discussing options for the fastest way across Aadya for Jewel to open the other portal.

"I think once we get home we should fly," said Coda.

"No, that is not a good idea," commented Anton.

"Why, it would be the fastest way to travel?" asked Coda.

"Because Morgana could see us. If she finds out that we are all back in Aadya she will try for the girls again. Also did you forget that Temprance is afraid of flying," said Anton.

"I agree that it would be the fastest way to travel but I will not make Temprance do anything she is not comfortable with. I bet Anton would agree with me if it were Acelyn afraid of flying," stated Zeke.

"What is it with you two? Now that you have mates you seem to have lost your brains. We fly so fast we would be where we need to be in no time," argued Coda.

"Coda, one day you will find your mate, then you will understand that you would do anything to make them happy or keep them safe," explained Anton.

"Now back to our problem, I think the best way across is walking, only because we can stay better hidden. Remember Aadya is still cursed which means Morgana, Kahn, or their spies would see us in no time. There are not even birds flying right now," said Zeke.

"But one big thing before anything is set in stone, we need to bring the girls in on this conversation. They are a part of this, they have a say in how things go," said Anton.

"Agreed," said the others in unison.

Walking into the kitchen Anton, Zeke, Coda, and Jaz just watched as the girls danced and sang while packing the bottomless bag.

"Hey Dove, is that the song you let me hear the other night?" Anton asked.

No longer embarrassed she turned toward the guys still dancing "Nope, this song is called The Shape of You by Ed Sheeran." Dancing over to Anton she grabbed his hands with a movie star smile "Come dance with me, my love."

"Any other time I would love to, but we have things to discuss plus we need to get moving. We will want to be in Aadya before night fall," said Anton lowering down to capture her lips in a kiss.

Pushing out her bottom lip she pouted just a little, "Okay I will let you get away with it just this one time," she said. Then turned and danced back to the girls to finish up. Turning to see if the guys were still there Temprance caught her by the arm, "I haven't had time to catch up with you. I do have to say you seem happy."

Acelyn's eyes started to glow just a little with her excitement, "Oh Tempie I am, Anton is an amazing person. I know I will be happy with him for a lifetime, I can just feel it."

"I am glad you are happy, and you have found someone that will love you as much as you do," said Temprance giving Acelyn a hug. "Now if we don't want them angry with us, we need to hurry ladies."

Acelyn, Temprance, and Jewel finished up and joined the guys once again under the pergola. "Okay, we are already, so what do we do now?" asked Acelyn walking over to Anton and plopping down onto his lap.

Looking up at the sky he spoke "Well it is about lunch time here, right?"

"Yes, but what does that have to do with the price of tea in China?" asked Temprance. She was met with five confused faces. All Acelyn could do is laugh at the look on Anton's face.

Coda was the first to speak, "What is a China?"

Between bouts of laughter Acelyn said, "It is not a what, it is a place." Well, there is a China that is a what, but in this case, it is a place. All Temprance meant, is what does the time here have to do with what we are going to talk about."

"Well, why did she not say that?" Coda asked in a huff.

"Because if she would have said it your way it would have lost the humor in what she was saying."

"I will never understand you and your sister's humor, Dove. The reason is when the sun is high in the sky here, the sun will be just rising in Aadya. So, if we hurry, we will have a full day to make it where we need to go," explained Anton.

The heroes stood and gathered their things while Jewel concentrated on opening the portal. The air in front of them shimmered, went white, then opened. Through the portal they could see a forest that was completely imprisoned in stone. One at a time they left Edan behind. Not knowing while they were planning their next move Morgana was two steps ahead.

Chapter Fourteen

Spike slept while Morgana prepared for the next step in her plan. "The only way I am going to get around those viper harpies is a disguise." Laughing to herself she started to work. Reaching up she pulled a stone out of the wall, reaching in she pulled out a small vial of blood. "There; this should work." Turning she stood in front of her caldron and chanted:

> *I call on the water of the sea I summon thee,*
> *I call on the hottest fire from the underworld I summon thee,*
> *Come and do my bidding I call to thee.*

The water filled the caldron and fire blazed below heating the water to boiling. Morgana started throwing in her ingredients, a heart of a bat, eyes of a lizard, wings of a bird, and last the vial of blood.

> *Mix and bubble so that I may do my evil,*
> *Weave my image so that I may look like he,*
> *So, mote it be.*

The potion went a dark blood red and the flames turned blue, there was a flash of light then everything went quiet. The flames died out and only red embers glowed. Morgana filled a vial with the potion knowing that it would only last a few hours. She put the vial in her pouch.

Morgana gathered the rest of the stuff she needed, calling to Spike she headed out once more. She headed northeast to the Emerald Sea, knowing there was a passageway under Poseidon's temple that would lead to the catacombs under the coliseum in Greece. Morgana bitched and complained, "With all the power I have and the one thing I need right now I cannot do. That is why I always needed Kahn, he could shift into a black panther and traveling was so much faster. I would still have Kahn on my side if Miss Queen Bitch would have died when I tried to kill her in the Shadow Realm. But no, he did not trust me and followed me. She will die too at my own hands."

Feeling a tiny bit better after her rant she stopped and planned how to get past that stupid bird. Coming up on the Dead Lands she had an idea. "Spike, go and distract the bird while I make my way across then come and join me." Running off, Spike started sniffing and pawing the ground challenging Malic.

Looking down at the pup Malic shook his head and ruffled his feathers. Turning his head and tucking it into his wing Malic started to go back to sleep. Spike stopped and looked back at Morgana, signaling him to continue. Spike stood on his back legs and pushed on the tree that Malic was perched on. Getting annoyed looking back at Spike he puffed out his chest and squawked hoping he would leave. With Spike being persistent and Malic getting pissed off, it gave Morgana the opening she needed to pass by. Malic had his talons deep in the side of the tree, and he stretched out trying to pluck one of its six eyes out. Suddenly Spike just stopped and ran away. "Stupid pup, how and the world did he get out of the underworld? Well Hades will be looking for him, enjoy your freedom while it lasts," said Malic trying to get comfy again. Then it dawned on him, that hell hound wanted to distract him, and it worked. Knowing he needed to find out what that pup was up to he would need help. Taking off he went in search for someone to help.

As Morgana crossed between realms the air made a popping sound. On the other side, Morgana was met with the musky smell that came from the wet, stone corridor that led into the catacombs. Taking the vial out of her pouch she smiled to herself and drank it. By drinking the potion, Morgana transformed herself to look and sound like Khan. Knowing she had a time limit, Morgana hurried through the maze, following the screeching voices coming from the harpies. When Morgana came to the door leading into the room that held the sleeping princess she stopped just outside and listened. Morgana checked for magic wards then she slammed the end of the staff on the ground three times then entered the room.

Looking at the harpies she snarled, "Get away from her!"

Flying over they bowed at her feet, "We are sorry master Kahn, we were just making sure your Queen's lineage was still breathing. We were only acting on your orders, my king."

"Well, I am here to take her, so your services are no longer needed. Go now, when I have use for you, I will send word."

The harpies looked at each other bowed once more and left. Morgana walked over to Zanderley and waived the staff over her. The protective shield vanished. Reaching in her pouch, Morgana pulled out a petrified vine. Saying her chant once more she turned the vine into a beautiful choker, it was black with silver filigree. The sapphires and diamonds sparkled like they were in the sun. Bending down she locked it around Zanderley's neck. Waiving the staff once more she woke the princess from her sleep. When her eyes opened Morgana spoke.

"Come, we must hurry, I have come to rescue you; it will not be long before they come back."

"Who are you?" asked Zanderley in a sleepy voice,

"We will have time to talk about that once we are safely away from here," said Morgana holding her hand out.

Taking Morgana's hand, Zanderley felt something was not quite right. "Where are my sisters? Why did they not come for me? And what happened to that tiny dragon that was helping me when that man attacked me?"

"Shh, my child I will explain everything when we are safe. Now we need to go," explained Morgana.

Morgana and Zanderley ran back through the maze to the portal that led to Aadya. Morgana crossed over first then Zanderley. Once the princess had both feet on the other side, the whole realm shook.

Chapter Fifteen

The sounds of cracking filled the skies, the ground rumbled and shook. Acelyn looked down and noticed that the ground was splitting where they stood. Grabbing her sister, she pulled Temprance to her side before the crack split any further.

"Hey, what was that for?" Temprance asked.

Pointing down, "Look, you were going to fall in."

Looking down Temprance watched as the split in the ground widened. Before anyone could comment or move, there was a loud explosion. Looking over where the sound came from, the heroes saw the top of the volcano start to spew out lava. Leaning down Acelyn picked a stone flower, cupping it in her hands she held it to her heart. With tears falling down her face she looked at Anton and said, "My uncle did all of this?"

"Yes, Dove."

"How could he be so heartless?"

Looking over at her sister Temprance said, "Remember what Mya told us that our uncle was evil before he was born. Morgana did that to him, so by default I don't think that Uncle Kahn can be held accountable." Looking around Temprance shook her head, "No, I blame this on Morgana. If there is anything that can be done, we will find a way to save him as well."

Pulling her hands away from her chest she lifted her hand and wiped the tears away, never noticing what she did to the flower. Looking down at her hand that was holding the flower Temprance gasped. Getting everyone's attention Zeke raced to her side.

"What is wrong Agape Mu?" asked Zeke

Unable to speak she just pointed to the flower in Acelyn's hand. Acelyn looked where her sister was pointing, without saying a word she lifted the Gerber Daisy to her nose and sniffed. Acelyn heard Anton say something but she could not make out what he said. Turning to face him the words never got a chance to pass her lips. Anton leaned down and kissed Acelyn on both cheeks then on her lips. Taking the flower from her he walked behind her and fixed the flower into the top of her braid. Speaking only loud enough for her to hear, "Welcome home, your Majesty." Turning quickly, she asked, "What made you say that Anton?"

"Because the curse is breaking."

"How do you know?" asked Temprance.

"It was told when the Princesses returned home that the world would shake and crumble, then the realm would be reborn," said Zeke.

The girls looked around and saw no sign of rebirth, so Temprance walked over to a tree and placed her hand on the trunk. When she lifted her hand, the spot was brown. Getting excited, she called to her sister. "Hey Ace, come over here I want you to see something." Acelyn quickly joined her sister, placing her hand over Temprance's the princesses closed their eyes and wished life back into the tree. Lifting their hands, the brown spot grew but the tree remained in stone. Joining them Jewel looked at Temprance and Acelyn, "You will need your sister to heal the realm."

Temprance and Acelyn turned and looked at Anton then looked back at the tree. Walking over to Anton, "How is this possible? What makes us so special?" asked Acelyn.

Reaching up to touch her face he spoke, "Because you and your sisters are the key to breaking the curse and saving us all. Also, it was your blood line that cursed this realm. So, my dear you and your sister are the only ones that can help us."

"Okay I get that but how is that possible?" asked Acelyn pointing at the tree.

"The only thing that would explain everything that is happening, the ground shaking, volcano being active, and the girls being able to make the stone fall away, must mean that Zanderley is in Aadya and not in Athens, Greece," stated Coda causing everyone to look his way.

In unison the girls yelled, "What? How?"

"Kahn must have moved her," said Jaz.

Shaking her head, "No, I don't think he would take a chance and move her now that Aunt Bella is with him," said Temprance.

"I agree with Temprance," said Jewel.

"Then there are only two other ways she could be here. One she escaped or two Morgana has her hidden," said Zeke.

"I would bet on Morgana has her. Only because if she were able to free herself how would she get here?" asked Acelyn.

As the group talked and figured out were to go next the girls started fanning themselves. Seeing the sweat run down Temprance's face Zeke walked over to her. Studying her closely he reached in the enchanted bag and pulled out a bottle of water and handed it to her.

"Temprance, are you feeling alright?" asked Zeke.

"Yes, I feel fine, but it is hot. Is the weather always like this?" asked Temprance while wiping the sweat off her face.

"I sure hope not," commented Acelyn. "Or we are going to figure out how to make the castle have central air."

Temprance laughed so hard she fell to her knees wrapping her arms around her middle. "Careful sis, you are starting to sound like me."

Already confused Anton chose not to ask what central air was, he walked over to the split in the ground. "Here is where your heat is coming from, lava has filled the cracks in the ground."

Jumping up Acelyn ran over to Anton to look. Before she could get to close, he grabbed her arm so she would not fall in. Looking down in the crack Acelyn saw the lava and with her eyes she traced the ground to see if she could see where it was coming from. Looking back up at Anton, "Hey transform and take me up in the air I want to see how far it goes."

"I do not think that is a good idea Dove, what if Morgana sees us?" asked Anton.

"Don't you think that she already knows we are here by the way the realm shook?" asked Acelyn.

"Yes, I guess you are correct."

"Good, now transform so I can go look."

Anton's form faded into a silver dragon. Acelyn was awestruck, when the sun hit his scales it looked like he was covered in millions of diamonds. Walking over to him she ran a hand down the broad side of his neck leaning in she rested her head on him. Anton turned and lowered his head, so his eyes were level with hers; very gently he rubbed his cheek against hers. Reaching out with both hands she cradled his face and kissed his snout. Even his rough voice sounded like silk when he spoke, "I love you, my Dove."

"I love you too, Anton."

Stepping away so he could lower his wing, Acelyn placed her foot in the crook between his wing and back and hoisted herself up. Once seated she looked over to her sister, "Tempie, do you want to go? Anton is taking me up so I can see how far the rivers of lava go?"

"Is he just taking you up?" asked Temprance.

"Yes, we are just going up high enough so we can see in the distance."

Coming over to join her sister Temprance climbed up the same as Acelyn. Once she was seated Anton took flight, once they were high enough, he stopped. Pointing over at the volcano Acelyn spoke, "Look, the cracks in the ground cover the whole realm. The lake of lava at the base of the volcano looks like a pulsing heart." Looking at the pattern of the cracks Temprance said, "Anton, take us down I need to tell the others something."

Anton landed and the girls slid off, then his form faded, and he walked back over to the group. Looking over to Temprance he asked, "Okay, what did you need to tell us?"

"The cracks spread all over Aadya and look like veins. The lava is such a deep color of red that it reminds me of blood. The lake at the base of the volcano is pulsing like a beating heart. I think the guys were right, Aadya has been reborn. Which means Zanderley is here. Now we just need to find her."

Chapter Sixteen

On the other side of the realm Nightwing and Ember race to the Cavern of the Fates. When the Realm shook it caused a sonic quake through the skies as well, causing Nightwing and Ember to spin out of control and fall to the ground. The only words spoke between the two was, "They are home!" Acting quickly, they took flight once more.

In the Firelands Mya was franticly searching for the fire orchid when the volcano erupted and the ground split. Spotting the rare flower Mya let out a sigh of relief until the ground gave away sending the flower to fall into the deep gorge. Acting on pure instinct Mya dove going after the flower, everything seemed to move in slow motion causing Mya to feel like she was moving through quicksand. Just before the orchid fell in the river of lava, she grabbed it and held it to her chest. Flying up to see what had happened and to assess the damage. She slowly flew in a circle and the only words she could utter were, "Welcome home."

Flying above keeping an eye on his beloved, Kane could see the opening to the cavern. Seeing the ground start to split, Kane landed and shifted. Running he picked up Catarina and took them out of harm's way. Setting Catarina down she shifted and smiled, wrapping her arms around him she squealed, "Kane, my love, you know what this means? They are here, the girls are home."

"Yes, they are home, but we cannot celebrate yet. There is still so much that needs to be done. Come on we need to get moving, because if the girls are home, we are running out of time." They were almost at the opening of the cavern when a boulder dropped in front of the door.

At the palace in between realms Bella and Kahn were sitting out in the garden. Kahn was watching Bella tend to her rainbow of roses when the echo of the aftershock hit. Letting out a snarl, "Impossible!" said Kahn.

"My girls did it, they made it home," whispered Bella.

Walking over to Bella he grabbed her by the arms and turned her to face him. When Bella looked Kahn in the eyes, she could see the rage in them, they were glowing a deep crimson red. "What did you say?"

Showing no fear, she stated louder "My girls made it home, they are in Aadya."

Kahn sneered and grabbed Bella's wrist "That is impossible, those brats would have never got past the harpies." Pulling her so she would follow him, "Come, I will show you." Grabbing his staff, he waived it in the air and opened a portal and pulled Bella through. Once through the portal Kahn let a growl that sent a chill up Bella's spine. Walking over to the stone tub that had water in it he summoned the harpies. The longer he waited the more upset Kahn got. He paced and grumbled to himself growing more impatient with each lap around the room.

Bella jumped at Kahn's yelling "It is about time! Where have you been and where is the princess?"

Bowing down the harpies shook as they spoke, "But you told us to leave, my lord. You took the princess with you when you came earlier."

"What is this nonsense you are speaking of? I was not here earlier I was with your queen at our castle," he spat.

Seeing the chaos about to unfold Bella walked up and stood next to Kahn and laid her hand on his arm to calm him. Looking down at the harpies she asked, "What do you mean Kahn came earlier and took the princess?"

But the harpies did not answer her. Bella could feel the rage roll off Kahn, "Your queen asked you a question, you will show her respect. Now bow before your queen!" Kahn bellowed.

The harpies shook as they moved to bow in front of Bella, feeling bad for the poor creatures she told them to stand, they stood but kept their heads bowed at a respectful angle. "Explain to me what happened earlier?

While waiting for the harpy to answer her she studied the creature. She was half human and half bird and stood four feet in height. With long black hair that draped over her shoulders. Her hands and feet were emerald green with razor sharp talons. Her body was covered with black feathers except for her stomach, chest, neck, and face. The skin was pale white. The wings were covered in black feathers with red tips. Bella focused on the harpy's eyes and teeth, she noticed that the spear like tail twitched as she spoke.

"Yes, my queen," she hissed. "Earlier Lord Kahn came and told us that he was moving the princess to keep a better eye on her. Then he dismissed us, and just before we left, he told us that if he needs anything we would be summoned."

As Bella talked, she noticed that the harpy's long pointy ears twitched while she listened. "Well, I am telling you that Kahn did not come and get Zanderley it was someone else. Did this imposter show any signs of being different?" asked Bella.

"No, my queen that is why we left because we thought it was Lord Kahn. If we had known that it was not, he, we would have destroyed the imposter."

Stepping forward showing the anger she felt, "Go and find my niece and bring her back safely to me. If you hurt one hair on her head, I will pluck out every feather and roast you over the fire for the kingdom's next feast. Do I make myself clear?"

"Yes, your majesty."

"Then go and do not come back without her!"

The harpies jumped back, let out a squawk, and flew out of the room. Bella closed her eyes trying to calm herself, she could feel Kahn just watching her and knew when he moved in front of her.

"Bella, my love, calm down; they will find her. When they do, she will be brought to the castle. If they harm her in any way, I will rip off their wings." Reaching down he gently gripped Bella's wrists, noticing the blood dripping from her fists she grasped. Kahn gently opened her hand one finger at a time. Seeing that her hand was covered in blood, he ripped a piece of his robe and wiped her hand clean. After seeing the damage Bella had done to her hand, he shook his head. While applying pressure to the wound he used his other hand and reached into his satchel and pulled out a bottle of salve, with a loving caress he tended her wounds.

Taking another piece of his robe he tied them around her hands. Once he was done tending to Bella's hands, he pulled her into his arms and cradled her head between his hand and chest. Just for a moment Bella could feel the old Kahn coming through. Closing her eyes once more she said a silent prayer, "I will save you, my love, if it is the last thing I do."

Chapter Seventeen

The heroes stood outside the walls that surrounded the royal estate not sure how they truly felt about going in. Acelyn grabbed Anton's hand and looked over at her sister. "Tempie, we were born here."

"Come on girls, you do not want to get caught out here when it is dark," said Zeke.

Looking up at the sky Jaz commented, "We better hurry the sun is setting."

"I know this sounds stupid, but it does not feel right going in the first time without Zanderley with us," said Temprance.

"Well, this is the safest place we can be in all of Aadya. Plus, there is no time to argue," said Coda making a move along gesture with his hands.

As they walked across the stone drawbridge the ground shook once more. Letting the girls walk ahead, the others watched as the stone crumbled and fell away, leaving behind what was imprisoned. When the group made it to the big double doors Anton stopped them before they could touch the doors.

"Temprance, Acelyn, wait; do not touch the doors."

Jumping back as if they had got bitten, the girls turned their heads, "What? Why?"

"We did not want to say anything just yet, but look down." Looking down the girls traced the cobble stone walk back to the drawbridge. Taking off at a run Temprance stopped just before the bridge started. Squatting down Temprance touched the dark oak, "How did this happen?" she asked looking over her shoulder.

Before anyone could answer there was a loud hissing sound. Without saying a word Anton and Zeke picked up the girls and ran for the castle.

"Zeke, what is going on you are scaring me? What was that sound?"

"Anton, I swear to the gods if you don't put me down, I am going to kick you in your dragon balls, and you will be singing soprano for a week."

"We will put you down once we are safely inside the castle," said Anton turning so that Acelyn could touch the door.

"Agape Mu, please do not fight me. Touch the door and once we are inside, I will explain," pleaded Zeke.

When Temprance and Acelyn touched the doors, the stone crumbled into dust and fell. The doors were the same dark oak as the drawbridge. Before they could inspect the doors, the guys pushed them open. "Quick, everyone in," yelled Coda. Once everyone was in Coda, Anton, and Zeke slammed the doors shut.

"Now tell me what in the hell is going on?" asked Acelyn.

"When you girls entered the realm, the curse weakened. Well, when the curse weakened it awoke evil nasty creatures. Kahn had put them in a deep sleep so if you girls made it this far, they would stop you. And that sound my dear princesses was a gorgon," explained Anton.

"Wait, so you're telling me that Medusa is outside of the castle?" asked Acelyn.

"Well not Medusa herself but a creature like her," said Coda.

"No Flippin Way! I want to see," commented Temprance trying to jump to see out the window.

Grabbing Temprance by the waist and pulling her away from the window, "I do not think so, miss curiosity, I do not fancy a mate that is incased in stone," Zeke said flatly.

The sound of hissing had gotten louder, squirming out of Zeke's hold Temprance ran back to the window and jumped. Looking down "Umm, guys there is not one gorgon down there. Try there is at least twenty or so, there is also minotaurs, Cyclopes, and a shit ton of harpies. Now how do you suggest we deal with those?" asked Temprance.

Jumping up to join her sister, Acelyn studied the creatures. Growing up she had always loved the minotaur. Half man, half bull their weapon of choice was a huge hammer. But after looking at them in real life she had lost all love for the creature. The giant cyclopes were all the way in the back, they were snarling and carrying a huge club. The gorgons were truly vile, half snake, half human. The snakes in their hair were hissing and snapping out hoping to bite anything they could. There were so many harpies, hovering just off the ground just waiting for the time to strike.

Sliding down to where her feet were firmly back on the floor, she pulled her sister out of the window. "Sis, I think we are screwed," said Acelyn.

"Hello, did you forget we traveled here with five dragons? They can handle it," said Temprance with a smile.

Shaking his head, "Sorry Temprance, we cannot. We can still be turned into stone," said Anton.

"You are telling me I am here with five dragons stuck in this castle. None of you can fight them?" she asked.

All the guys shook their head no. "Oh shit, yep we are royally screwed," said Temprance.

"Maybe not," said Jewel with a smile then she started to chant:

Oh, goddess Artemis hear our plea,
Please come and help us
So, mote it be.

There was a flash of light and a popping sound and there stood Artemis in her battle armor. All Acelyn and Temprance could do was stare. Walking over to the princesses, Artemis laid a hand on each cheek, "Welcome home, your majesty." Then Artemis bowed, when she stood back up, she walked over to Jewel and hugged her friend. Still unable to speak, the girls just watched. Artemis looked at her friend and said with a wicked smile, "You have a problem here, let the hunt begin."

Chapter Eighteen

Artemis walked over to Acelyn and handed her a leather sheath. It was a rich chestnut brown with black around the edges. Taking the sheath from Artemis, Acelyn looked at the strange writing burned into the leather. "What does 'Makrys Zo o Vasilissa' mean?"

With a warm smile Artemis bowed "Long Live the Queen."

Reaching into the enchanted bag Anton pulled out her short sword and knelt. Laying the blade across both hands he held it up to Acelyn with his head bowed.

Elbowing her sister in the side, "Take the sword, Ace." Acelyn reached out and picked up the sword by the hilt and slid it into the sheath. Standing, Anton took the sword and sheath from her and showed her how to fasten it around her waist.

"Pretty snazzy, sis now all you need is battle armor," said Temprance.

Zeke walked over behind Temprance and wrapped his hands around her waist. "You will find yours soon, my love."

"Well, I sure hope it is not a sword or I am screwed," Temprance said with a laugh. Walking over to Temprance, "No, my child a sword is not for you," said Artemis. Reaching across her chest she gripped the bow what was hung across her body. With the other hand she took off the quiver of arrows, Artemis held them out for Temprance to take.

Temprance reached out and took the bow from Artemis, she could feel the magic within. Temprance watched as a bright light burnt something in the handle of the bow. Taking a closer look, it said Temprance Queen of Aadya.

Looking up at Artemis Temprance asked, "Where did you find this bow?" With a satisfied smile Artemis explained, "This bow has served me well for thousands of years. It will now serve you for as long as you reign. This bow was carved out of a branch from the Great Tree in the Enchanted Forest. The string is made from the hair of a unicorn." Temprance looked up at Artemis with a horrified look on her face. "Do not worry princess, the animal was not harmed." Letting out a sigh of relief she looked back down at the bow. On the hand grip it had black leather strips that were braided, in the center was the softest fur. Looking back up at Artemis, but before she could speak, she handed her the quiver full of arrows.

"The arrows are made from the same tree and the feathers are from a very special phoenix." Draping the bow diagonally across her chest she took out one of the arrows to inspect it. Temprance ran her hand up the arrow to the feathers.

"You said these feathers are from a phoenix, but they are black. The only phoenix I have seen have been colorful."

"Yes, these come from the black phoenix."

"Oh, I have never heard of a black phoenix before. I would like to see one, are there many?"

"No there is only one, he is the guardian of the Dead Lands and keeper of the dead," Artemis explained. "You will meet him eventually."

Temprance gave the feather one last stroke then placed it back in the quiver. She noticed that it was the same color as Acelyn's sword sheath, but it was sewn together with strands of gold thread. Running her hand down the Greek carving she read, "Makrys Zo o Vasilissa." Zeke reached over and took the bow from across her body and placed the quiver in its place. Leaning down he kissed her cheek then replaced the bow back where it was.

"Okay so these weapons are nice, but they don't help us in the current situation," said Acelyn pointing at the doors.

"Yes, they do, you needed them for the battle."

"Um, I sure as hell hope you don't think we are going out there," commented Acelyn.

"This is your fight; I am just here to help you. Your new weapons will keep you from being turned into stone. I will place a charm on all the dragons that will help as well. Now princesses what do you say, is it not time for you to start fighting for your people, your realm, and your home."

The girls looked at each other then back at Artemis and nodded. "Let's do this, what is our plan of action?" asked Acelyn.

Looking at the group, "We will need to head to one of the towers look-outs, follow me," said Artemis before taking off at a run.

The heroes followed Artemis as she weaved throughout the castle. When they reached the tower Artemis wanted, they climbed to the very top. Reaching the door at the top Artemis looked back, "Okay girls, you are up." Walking past Artemis, the princesses placed their hands on the door and watched in wonder, as the stone crumbled and fell away. Pushing the door open they walked out onto the roof. Temprance and Acelyn looked at what awaited them.

"You expect us to fight that!"

Chapter Nineteen

Walking over to join the girls Anton, Zeke and Coda looked at the army that awaited to tear them apart. Looking back at Artemis, Temprance shook her head, "You are frickin crazy lady. There is no way in hell we can fight that," she said while pointing.

"Temprance! Careful on how you speak to her she is a God. She could smite your ass out of existence." Stepping in front of Temprance to protect her just in case. "I am so sorry; she just means that...."

Giving Zeke a swift kick in the ass Temprance scolded him, "Zeke, I am a big girl and I meant that just how it sounded."

Tipping her head back Artemis let out a bellow of laughter. "I sure like how bold you are, princess. But Zeke is correct if you would have spoken to any other god like that, you would have been winked out of existence. So be mindful princess, of who and how you are speaking. Just show a little respect. Also, I said I was going to help you. We need to get started. I need all of the dragons to transform."

Walking over to stand next to Artemis the girls watched the dragons transform. They were breath-taking, their colors were so vibrant in the rising sunlight. When Zeke shifted Temprance's breath caught in her lungs. He looked so different. His scales were now a deep midnight black, the under skin on his wings were now white. Walking over to him she felt the rest of the world fall away. She was lost in his luminescent blue eyes.

Acelyn seemed to be frozen in time when she looked at Anton because she could see her reflection in his scales. When Anton stretched out his wings, she noticed that the webbing underneath his wings were now a dark gray. Acelyn walked over to him and went to her favorite place, she nestled herself in between his front shoulder and the crook of his neck. Laying her head down she let out a long-satisfied sigh.

Jaz stood tall and proud next to Jewel; they both held their heads high. Looking over at Jaz, Acelyn stood up and yelled to her sister. "Hey, Temprance look at Jaz and Jewel." Looking down at the dragons "Holy shit, Jaz, you have feathers on your wings." Jaz turned his head and looked at his wings. Not only did he have feathers they were a mix of brown, green, light, and dark purple. Looking over at Jewel her wings matched his, Jaz turned his head so he could nuzzle her jaw with his snout.

Acelyn looked over at Coda his scales were a brilliant cobalt blue. But there were no changes in Coda's colors, his whole body was the same shade. Grabbing her sister by the arm she pulled her until they were over next to Artemis. "Why hasn't Coda's colors changed, the rest have?" asked Acelyn.

"Because he has not found his mate yet. When dragons find their mate, they will change so that a little piece of their mate will be shown. Zeke, the part of his wings is now white. The under part of Anton's wings is now a dark gray. The same with Jaz and Jewel they now wear each other's colors. I am sure when Coda and Zanderley find each other and bonded he will wear a color to represent her."

Looking back at all the dragons Acelyn leaned over and whispered to Temprance, "Tempie, they are our family now."

"I know the only one missing is Zanderley," said Temprance frowning.

"I promise Tempie, we will find her and bring her home. She is a part of this family even if she does not know it yet. We will win this war and take back our home. Just like our parents wanted us to, we are going to live long happy lives and have lots of babies. But the best part of all of this is that I have found where I belong." Looking over at Artemis she smiled, "but now it is time for us to kick some ass. So, what do you say sister do we hide? Or do we fight to live another day so we can have the lives we wanted?" asked Acelyn.

Temprance looked her sister in the eyes and could see the determination and truth in what she said. "Fight, I want to fight."

"Okay girls, if you are ready to accept your destiny, let us begin." Artemis's eyes turned bright white and she reached to the sky and called to her father Zeus for the strength and lightning. Out of nowhere a lightning bolt came from the sky, Artemis caught the bolt in one hand.

She put her arms out to the sides and looked to the heavens. Slowly she lifted her hands and cupped the bolt between them to make a glowing orb. Holding the orb in front of her Artemis started to float off the ground. When she was about three feet above the dragons, she spoke in ancient Greek. While she spoke, she pulled her hands apart making the orb split into five. By the time she was done speaking an orb hovered over each dragon.

Acelyn and Temprance watched Artemis as she did her ritual. Just before Artemis finished saying her spell her body was ingulfed in a bright white light. The morning sky had gone black as night with storm clouds, the girls watched as the clouds parted to show Zeus. Zeus held a bolt of lightning in his left hand, letting it go the bolt split into five smaller bolts. Temprance and Acelyn held their breath when they noticed the lightning headed straight for the dragons.

When the bolt hit the orbs there was an explosion of light that sent a shockwave sending the girls flying back. When the light receded, the dragons had battle armor on. On the backs of Zeke, Anton, and Coda there were saddles that were meant for battle. The girls noticed that the saddles matched their weapons. Taking a deep breath Temprance walked over to Zeke, she ran a hand down his neck and side until she reached the saddle. Calming herself she grabbed a hold of the saddle and climbed up. Looking over at her sister she noticed that Acelyn was already seated and ready to hear the battle plan. Taking one more second to calm herself she smiled at the voice that entered her head.

"Agape Mu, I love you. I will not let anything happen to you."

"Zeke my love, for some reason I just feel this is right. I am not scared anymore, I will be okay," said Temprance as she leaned down to rub his neck.

Once everyone was situated Artemis went over the battle plan. "Temprance and Zeke you will take care of the minotaurs. Acelyn and Anton you go take out the gorgons, Coda, Jaz, and Jewel you work on the harpies. I will deal with the cyclops, remember to help each other, you are more powerful as a team."

After Artemis was done, she put both pinky fingers in her mouth and let out an ear-piercing whistle. The sound of thunder cracked and from the skies came a pure black Pegasus that left flames in its wake. When he flew past the princesses, they could feel the heat from the flames. When he landed the stone cracked. He walked up to Artemis and nudged her shoulder with his massive head. Climbing down from the dragons the girls walked up to him. The feathers on his wings were black and red. His coat was so black he looked almost a deep purple. Reaching up Acelyn asked if she could pet the massive beast. Nodding her head yes, Acelyn reached up and pet his mane and neck. "His mane feels like silk," commented Acelyn.

Temprance leaned in for a closer look at his eyes, "Are those flames?" she asked. Looking down she also noticed the flame dancing around his hoofs. Still stroking his neck, "What is his name, Artemis?"

"His name is Tidius, he belongs to my uncle Hades. I take him whenever I go hunting or out to battle, when my uncle is not fighting."

"He is beautiful," the girls said in unison.

With a small jump Artemis vaulted up onto Tidius's back. Temprance noticed that Artemis did not have a weapon, "Artemis, where is your weapon?"

"Weapon, I do not need a weapon," said Artemis.

"What do you mean you don't need a weapon?" asked Acelyn climbing back in the saddle.

Temprance and Acelyn watched Artemis dig her heals into the sides of Tidius making him raise up on his back legs. Tipping her head back she laughed, when she looked back at the princesses her blue eyes were gone. They were all white and you could see the sparks in them. "Remember girls, I am a god," said Artemis. When Tidius's front hoofs contacted the stone on the floor of the tower it caused the castle to shake.

As Temprance and Acelyn got secure in the saddles, Artemis held Tidius's reins tight causing him to dance in place. Once they were all ready Tidius snorted black smoke while he pawed the ground causing the flames around his hoofs to dance. The girls could feel the anticipation coming from Anton and Zeke. Reaching down they stroked their necks. Out of the blue Acelyn yelled "Okay Artemis, let's hunt." That was all Artemis needed, she gave slack in Tidius's reins and he took off. When they got to the end of the walk, he opened his wings and took flight.

Acelyn felt so powerful sitting on the back of Anton she knew when he was ready to take flight. His muscles rolled and tightened, then they were in the air. Worried about her sister she looked over at Temprance and her mouth fell open.

Chapter Twenty

Temprance was standing in the saddle on Zeke's back with her bow drawn. Every arrow that she released hit its mark. She looked every bit of a warrior queen. Looking around for the others she saw Jaz, Jewel, and Coda doing their part in fighting the harpies. Acelyn heard a loud cry of pain, she turned in her saddle to see what happened. She noticed that a harpy had laid open Coda's left hip. Jaz and Jewel raced to help him, they each grabbed opposite ends of the harpy and pulled it in half. Acelyn shuttered at the sight below her, the ground was riddled with dead creatures and blood.

Acelyn's heart pounded because she knew that she needed to start fighting soon. Drawing her sword, she said, "Okay my love, let's get these bastards." As soon as the words left her lips, Anton dove for the ground. Once the first gorgon was in sight Acelyn closed her eyes screamed and swung, hitting her mark severing its head from the body. Acelyn heard Anton's soothing voice, "Well done Dove, next time try it with your eyes open, you almost clipped me with your sword. Scared she would hurt him, the next time she swung she kept her eyes open. Starting to feel impowered she got bolder and raised to her knees in the saddle.

Acelyn heard a dragon howl and Temprance yell. The next thing she saw made her heart stop. Acelyn saw Temprance falling to the ground, she knew that she would never get to her sister in time. Then a miracle happened about twenty feet from the ground, Temprance's form faded. Landing on all fours, Temprance let out a roar that shook the ground. Taking off she ran and leaped onto a minotaur's back making it fall face first. Temprance bit down on the minotaur's head with her powerful jaw while placing her massive paws on its shoulders, then Temprance turned her head and snapped its neck. Deciding she was going to help her sister she told Anton to take her down. She put her sword back in its sheath and hung the belt on the saddle. Once she was close enough, she stood and jumped and shifted forms. Landing on all fours she also let out a roar and started to prowl. Looking up at Anton she spoke to him telepathically, "Go and help Zeke my love, Temprance and I have things down here." Then she ran to aid her sister in the fight

Anton flew over to Zeke and together they each took a gorgon; they positioned themselves that when they landed their claws dug in the torso knocking it down. They bit down on the head and ripped it from the bodies. Spitting out the heads they roared sending out jets of flames burning anything in its path. Acelyn saw that there was a harpy coming straight for Temprance. Acting quickly, she jumped and pulled the winged beast out of the sky and crushed its throat with her powerful jaws. At the sound of a battle cry, the heroes looked to the sky and saw Artemis and Tidius take the blow that sent them crashing to the ground. They all took off for the cyclops, the closer they got the bigger it was. Acelyn and Temprance jumped and sank their claws into its upper legs, knocking it back so it would not stomp on Artemis. Tidius took flight once more to join the fight, once he was high enough, he kicked it in the eye.

Jaz and Jewel stayed on the ground to tend to Artemis. Jewel nudged her with her muzzle, but nothing happened. Jewel shifted into her human form and knelt next to her friend. Looking up at Jaz she spoke, "Jaz, can you heal her?"

Jaz looked down at Jewel and said, "I can try. She is a god I have no idea if it will work." Jaz took a step back and flapped his wings and took a deep breath, when he breathed fire it was the whitest flames that Jewel had ever seen. They engulfed Artemis completely, sticking out her hand she wanted to feel the heat from the fames but there was none. By the time Jaz was done he collapsed, taking a minute to catch his breath he lifted his head and looked at Artemis. But there was still no change, shifting to human form he knelt on the other side of the goddess. Not knowing what to do they watched the rest of the battle while keeping Artemis safe.

Jaz looked out over the battlefield and noticed that the only thing left standing was the cyclops that the others were fighting. Jewel shifted to where she could lay Artemis's head in her lap and watch the others. She watched as

Temprance and Acelyn climbed up the cyclops leaving bloody gashes behind them. The giant cyclops swung his huge club at Zeke and hit a line of trees breaking them in half. On the next swing he clipped Zeke and sent him spiraling down to the ground. Anton and Coda bit him in the shoulder causing it to scream in pain. They tried to pull the cyclops backwards, but it still had balance. Zeke shook his head and took flight once again, back in the air he sent a jet of black flames at the cyclops's club rendering it to ash.

As Jewel and Jaz watched, they worried for their family. Like he had been struck by lightning he jumped up and sent a message telepathically to the others. "One of you need to ram him in the chest while the other two aim for the back of his knees," said Jaz.

Zeke told the girls to climb down and get to safety so that when the cyclops fell it would not fall on them. After the girls were down Acelyn noticed that Jewel was holding something in her lap. Temprance and Acelyn ran as fast as they could, they weaved around dead creatures. Once they were close, they skidded to a stop and shifted back to their human forms. The girls knelt around Artemis, Acelyn put an ear to her chest and let out the breath she was holding. "She is alive, she is just knocked out," explained Acelyn. Turning around to watch the others, Zeke, Anton, Coda, and Tidius flew in a circle making the cyclops turn. Once they had him in the spot, they wanted the guys flew away. Zeke let out a roar and they all flew at once, Coda and Anton hit at the same time making the cyclops knees buckle. Then Zeke flew as fast as he could to make the impact hit harder. Zeke's aim was dead on, he hit the cyclops in the middle of the chest sending the cyclops to fall backwards.

The cyclops landed on one of the broken trees, it impaled him in the chest killing it instantly. Flying down to the others, the princes shifted once they landed. Anton went to Acelyn's side and knelt by her, Zeke went and stood behind Temprance, Coda knelt next to Jaz, and the heroes just watched the sleeping goddess. Tidius pawed the ground and lowered his head down over Jewel and he nuzzled the side of Artemis's face. There was still no response from the sleeping beauty. Anton surveyed their surroundings and watched the shadows very closely. Then he spoke, "I think we need to take Artemis in the castle, we are too open and vulnerable out here." Placing her hand on his bicep Acelyn suggested, "Anton, I agree with you, I have an idea to get her to the castle. Transform. I can hold on to her while you fly us to the castle."

"Hey, that is a good idea, sis," said Temprance.

Anton nodded, then he stood and walked away from the group and shifted. Zeke, Coda, and Jaz lifted Artemis and carried her over to Anton and waited for Acelyn to climb up and get seated. Anton used his wing to help the guys lift Artemis up and lay her across the saddle. Acelyn sat behind the saddle and held on to Artemis. Once they were settled Anton took flight. Jaz shifted and flew on one side and Jewel used her wings and flew on the other side of Anton to help if Artemis started to slide off. Before Zeke could transform, Tidius nudged Temprance in the back. Turning around she looked at the beautiful creature, and she noticed that he had his head bowed. Walking over to him she gave him a soft stroke on his neck, then the beautiful beast knelt offering Temprance a ride.

Temprance looked over at Zeke, he smiled and nodded, walking over she ran a hand down his neck. Just when she was about to jump and climb up, she felt Zeke's hands around her waist and lift her onto Tidius's back. Once she was seated, he did not move, leaning down Temprance asked. "Tidius, do you want Zeke to ride as well?" He neighed and bobbed his head up and down. "I think he wants you to ride, Zeke," commented Temprance. Taking the invitation Zeke vaulted up onto Tidius's back. As soon as Zeke was seated, he wrapped an arm around Temprance's waist and whispered into her ear, "Agape Mu, you scared the hell out of me when you jumped off my back. But you were so beautiful and fierce you looked every bit the warrior queen. I take it you are no longer scared of flying. Before she could answer Tidius reared up on his hind legs. Once his hooves landed back on the ground, he took off running causing a squeal to escape out of Temprance. Then the mighty beast opened his wings and took flight.

Chapter Twenty-One

Tidius circled around the castle twice before landing on the roof, he walked up next to the others. Tidius tried to nudge Artemis again, but there was no response. Zeke slid from Tidius's back and lifted Temprance down. They joined the others with Tidius behind them. The guys lifted Artemis from Anton's back and once Acelyn was on the ground Anton's form faded back to his human form.

Anton walked back over to the group and suggested, "Let us take her inside where it is safe. Then we can figure out what to do."

Nodding, Zeke, Coda, and Jaz bent down and picked up Artemis. Zeke was holding her shoulders, Coda and Jaz took the sides and Anton held her feet. Acelyn ran and opened the door for the guys and Temprance followed in. Acelyn turned back and looked at Tidius, he hung his head, and his wings were sagging. Feeling sorry for him Acelyn walked over to him, reaching up she pet his neck.

Speaking softly, she talked to him, "You are worried about her huh, big guy? Tell you what fly down to the front doors and I will let you in. You are just too big to fit down the stairs."

Getting excited Tidius stomped his feet and danced in place. Acelyn giggled, "Now hurry." Then she turned and ran for the door, at the doorway she turned back just in time to see him take off, shaking her head she shut the door and ran downstairs. Running like a bat out of hell, Acelyn headed for the front door. Temprance caught Acelyn out of the corner of her eye, without saying anything she turned and ran after her sister. Temprance heard Acelyn fighting with the front doors of the castle and went to find out what she was doing.

"Um, Ace, what are you up to?" asked a confused Temprance.

While yanking on the door she answered, "Trying...to...open...this...damn...door." Giving up in frustration she looked back at Temprance. "Are you going to help me or just stand there?"

Rolling her eyes Temprance went over to help, after a few good tugs the door opened and Temprance jaw dropped. "You are not letting him in here, are you?" asked Temprance.

Pushing her sister out of the way, "Yes, I am, he is worried about Artemis, so I am letting him in so he can be by her side."

"Ace, you can't be serious he is a horse with flames on his feet. This is going to be our home, what are you going to do if he burns it down? Huh, answer me that," said Temprance with a baffled look on her face.

"Temprance, yes this is going to be our home, and he is my guest, so help me or get out of my way," stated Acelyn while pushing the door open enough so Tidius could get in.

Once Tidius was in the castle Acelyn and Temprance fought to get the door to close. Tidius came over and put his head on the door and helped them push. The door closed with a loud thud.

"You know sis, the guys are going to give us hell for letting a horse in the castle," stated Temprance.

"Let them," was all she said. Acelyn walked over to Tidius and pet his neck once more. Speaking softly, she talked to him, "Hey big guy, do me a favor please stay away from anything that can catch on fire," then she leaned in and kissed his nose.

Tidius shook his head and the flames went out in his eyes, now they were a dark red. Then he stomped his left hoof three times, and the flames went out around his hooves. Giving her a whinny, he tucked his wings in tight to his body and waited for the princesses to show him the way. Walking through the castle the girls looked at the walls and wondered.

"Do you wonder what it would have been like growing up here with our parents?" asked Temprance.

"Yes, but I think that us growing up the way we did will help us be better Queens," said Acelyn.

"Yeah, how so?"

"Because think about it, Tempie. We will have the knowledge from both worlds," said Acelyn with a smile.

Walking closer to her sister Temprance draped an arm over her shoulders. "So, what are you going to tell the guys when they see Tidius?" asked Temprance.

"I will tell them the same thing I told you."

Walking into the throne room the girls noticed they had everyone's attention. The room went quiet as a tomb, then in slow motion the room exploded with sound. But there was one voice Acelyn heard over all of them, "Dove, what the hell is he doing in the castle?" asked a flabbergasted Anton. Seeing the flash of anger in Acelyn's eyes he decided to try a different approach. After walking over to Acelyn he reached out with a tentative hand and laid it on her arm. "Dove, I love you. But what is Tidius doing in the castle?"

Letting some of the anger in her eyes die a little she answered, "Because he was worried about Artemis. So, I told him that he could come in, plus is this not my home?" asked Acelyn raising an eyebrow.

"Yes, Acelyn this is our home, but...."

"But nothing," said Acelyn cutting him off. Reaching up she stroked Tidius's neck. "Come on big guy, let's go check on her." Then she just walked away from Anton. Anton turned and looked at Temprance. All Temprance could do for an answer was shrug her shoulders and went up to her sister. As he watched the princesses walk away, he hung his head in defeat and joined the others. Zeke leaned over and asked what was up with the animal in the castle, all Anton could do is lift his hands and shake his head.

Hours went by and there was no change in Artemis, Acelyn looked around at everyone and noticed almost everybody was asleep. Zeke was sitting on the floor with his back against a throne with Temprance's head in is lap. Tidius was laying on the floor with Jaz and Jewel using him as a pillow. Coda was talking with Anton softly and they were looking out over the battlefield. Acelyn was sitting with her legs under her next to Artemis who was laying on a bed made from pillows. Speaking just loud enough to where Anton could hear her. "Anton, do you think we should try and call Apollo or maybe Zeus?" she asked. "She has been like this for hours, plus we need to find some food for everyone."

Squatting down so he was almost eye level with Acelyn, he ran a hand down the back of her head stopping at her shoulders to play with her curls. "If you want to call for someone, I would call for Zeus."

Looking up at Anton she nodded then closed her eyes and chanted:

Oh, hail to the Gods hear my plea,
Please send Zeus to aid us in this hour of need,
So, mote it be.

Looking back up at Anton she asked, "Do you think he heard me?" Just as soon she got done speaking there was a loud popping sound and a blinding flash of light. Anton's eyes got wide and he dropped to one knee bowing before Zeus. The noise woke up Tidius. When he saw Zeus, he stood up causing Jaz's and Jewel's heads to hit the floor. They yelled causing the others to wake.

"Hey what is it with all the ruckus?" asked Zeke. When he noticed what was the cause he slowly got to his feet and joined Anton. Shortly after Coda, Jewel, and Jaz joined the guys.

"Sorry for bothering you, Zeus, but we did not know what to do," said Acelyn looking down at Artemis. "She has been like this for hours and we do not know how to help her."

Dropping to one knee next to his daughter he placed a hand on the top of her head and looked at the group. "You did right by calling for me, she needs to be in Mount Olympus. She needs the ether in the air for her body to heal." Looking over at his brother's winged beast he asked, "Who had the bright idea to let Tidius in the castle?" he asked.

Speaking up proudly Acelyn spoke, "It was my idea. He was worried about Artemis so I told him he could come in."

Zeus tipped his head back and laughed so loud it shook the castle. "Your mother was right, young queen. You and your sisters are just what Aadya needs."

Gripping her sister's hand Temprance spoke up, "You have spoken to our mother?"

"Yes, I have spoken to her and your father. They are both alive and well," said Zeus.

"Where are they? Can we see them? Do they know that Zanderley was taken?" asked Temprance and Acelyn in unison.

All Zeus did was nod, confused the girls were about to ask more questions when the sweetest voice came from behind them.

"Oh, Alex, look they are so beautiful."

90

Acelyn and Temprance jumped to their feet and turned and looked upon the faces of their parents for the first time. Temprance and Acelyn stood still as statues for in fear if they moved the vision in front of them would disappear. Anastasia could no longer take it, so she opened her arms welcoming them to her. With tears streaming down their faces, they ran almost knocking Anastasia over. Once she had the girls wrapped in her arms, Alexzander leaned down and kissed Temprance and Acelyn on the head. Not wanting to let go the girls squeezed just a little tighter.

Looking over her daughters heads she spoke, "Thank you, Zeus. I think my girls needed their mother." Looking down and resting her cheek on Acelyn's head. "I know I sure needed them. Now all we need is Zanderley and we will be complete," said Anastasia.

"I would like to thank you, young queens, for taking care of my daughter in her time of need. Because you have done this, I will do something for you. Your sister is in the Desiccated Woods. She is with Morgana, now I cannot go after her, but I can get her a message. Letting her know that her sisters are on their way," said Zeus bending down and picking up Artemis. He turned and started to walk away then turned back. "I suggest you sleep the night and get some rest. But before you do, eat and enjoy this small victory." Looking at Tidius he asked, "Are you coming with me or staying here with the princesses?" and then Zeus looked back at the heros and with a wave of his hand a banquet table full of food appeared.

The girls turned to say thank you, but Zeus and Tidius were already gone. Looking up at the celling both Temprance and Acelyn yelled thank you, sending the whole throne room into laughter. Looking around the room Acelyn searched for Anton, she found him standing with the others. Grabbing her mother's hand, she said, "Come with me there are some people we would like to introduce you to." Temprance followed suit and grabbed Alexzander's hand and pulled him along as well.

Chapter Twenty-Two

By the time they got over to the others, Coda, Anton, Zeke, Jewel, and Jaz were on one knee bowing. Anastasia looked at the group of people that had helped get Temprance and Acelyn this far and would also help rescue Zanderley.

"Rise all of you, there is no need to bow, I am no longer your Queen," said Anastasia with a warm smile. They all rose to their feet at the same time. She walked over to Coda, Anton, and Zeke and kissed them each on the cheek. "It is good to see you again, brave princes," Anastasia commented.

As soon as the words left her lips, Coda hung his head in shame. Turning to face him she cupped his face and lifted his head so she could look in his eyes. Anastasia noticed that he was barely able to hold back the tears.

"Why all the tears, sweet prince?" she asked

"Because I have failed you, I was not there to protect Zanderley and now she is prisoner to Morgana," said Coda sadly.

"That was not your fault Coda, when going through portals it can happen. Plus, you are going after her, correct?" Anastasia asked.

"Oh, yes, your majesty. I will not rest until I find her and bring her home," said Coda.

"Then no more of this sadness, this is a night of celebration, you all fought an army today and won."

The girls spoke up "Plus, Mom, if it was not for Coda helping Jaz, the four of us would have died," they said in unison.

Alexzander's eyes flashed with anger stepping up he asked, "What do you mean you would have died?"

"Alex, my heart, there will be time to catch up once we sit down to eat, let us finish with the introductions," Anastasia scolded.

Causing the girls to giggle, Acelyn leaned over to her sister and said, "Tempie, they are wonderful." All Temprance could do is nod in agreement.

Anastasia shifted so she was in front of Anton and Zeke, she noticed very quickly how her girls were clinging to the dragon princes. But little did they know Alexzander noticed as well. He made a mental note to talk to the dragons just to let them know he was watching, so if they had an idea to run off with his girls.

"Zeke, it has been so long. We missed you around the castle after Malic died. I am so glad you found your way back to us. Anton, I know your parents, and I am looking forward to getting to know you," said Anastasia. She turned and walked down to Jaz and Jewel. Opening her arm wide, Jewel ran to her dear friend and embraced her in a hug and they wept.

Confused the girls just looked at each other then back at their mother and Jewel. What seemed to take forever they stopped weeping. "Oh Jewel, I am so glad you are safe. I was afraid you did not escape the curse. But how did you get away? And how in the thirteen kingdoms did you end up with my daughters?" asked Anastasia.

"Well, that is a long story for another time. I promise Annie, we will catch up, but first I would like you to meet my mate and future king of the pixie dragons, this is Jaz," Jewel said proudly.

Bending down Anastasia cupped his face and kissed both of his cheeks. "Thank you, brave dragon, for saving my children's lives. I owe you a favor for keeping them safe and bringing them home to me and their father," she said.

Jaz stood proud and stated, "No disrespect, but you owe me nothing. It has been an honor helping Temprance and Acelyn. In the morning when they head out, I will be by their side. We will bring home Zanderley, your majesty, we are not just a group of people that are on a mission. We are a family, and I would gladly give my life's blood to protect them."

Smiling she stood back up, "You are a brave little dragon, Mya must be proud." Speaking loudly so everyone could hear, "Let us eat, we do not have much time before we need to head back." Seeing the faces of her daughters drop she walked over to them. "Do not be sad, we need to get back to Mount Olympus. But your father and I will always be there when you need us the most. When this war is over and won, we will have plenty of time together. I look forward to spending time with my three girls. Now let us eat, you need to rest," said Anastasia leading her girls to the table.

While the heroes ate their victory feast the harpies reported back to Bella and Kahn at the palace between realms. Bella sat in her throne next to Kahn when a knock sounded.

"Enter," was all Kahn said. The harpies flew to the steps before the thrones and knelt.

"We bring news," they hissed.

Before Kahn could answer Bella sat forward, "Speak, and if I do not like what you have to say to me, I will pluck out your feathers one by one," Bella spat. Waiting for the creature to answer she could only think about her sweet girl, and where could she be.

"The princess is with Morgana, my queen."

Moving fast, Bella was off her throne and grabbed the harpy by the neck. "What do you mean she is with Morgana. I told you not to come back here without her. Why did you not go and get her?" asked Bella.

Careful not to scratch or hurt Bella, the harpy tried to pry Bella's hand from around her neck. The harpy was barely able to squeak out an answer, "Because my queen, she has a new hell hound. We did try, but we could not get close enough." Bella loosened her grip just enough that the harpy could get free. As the harpy pulled her neck out of Bella's hand, she noticed that the queen had a bluish green ball of flames in her other hand. The harpy scrambled back and bowed as low as she could go at Bella's feet.

Kahn watched his queen in confusion, he knew he should be happy to see this kind of anger and aggression coming from his beloved. He found himself getting up and walking over to her. Kahn picked up her hand with the fireball and placed it between his, causing her to snap out of the haze of fury that she was caught in. As Bella calmed down, she noticed that Kahn had his eyes trained on her, it took her breath away at what she saw. Kahn's eyes we back to his normal black, startled by what she was seeing she shivered and looked back at the harpy.

Horrified at what she saw she tried to step back, but Kahn held her in place, so the harpies did not see it as a sign of weakness. Holding on to her hand with his left he stepped closer to her side and placed his right hand on her lower back so she could not retreat any further. Bella watched as the harpies shook with fear, finding her strength she spoke.

"Stand before me." Bella gasped when she saw the purpling mark grow around the harpy's neck. Khan could feel Bella's fear grow so he looked down upon the winged beast and felt sorry for the poor creature. After clearing his throat, he asked, "Are you certain that there was no way to get to the princess?"

Peeking a look at Bella before speaking she answered, "Yes my lord, there was no way to get to the princess," she hissed.

"Tell me everything," Kahn commanded. Then Kahn turned Bella around and led her back to the throne, when they were seated, he waived his hand for the harpy to continue.

"Well, after the Queen told us to find her, we searched the tunnels and found a potion bottle. So, we sniffed it to see if we could notice anything familiar, and we did. The smell of sulfur and wet dog, so we followed the sent and it led us to a portal, and it took us to the Emerald Sea. So, as we flew around trying to find the trail again, we remembered that only two people always have the smell of sulfur around them. That would be the lord of the underworld or Morgana. We did not think that the lord Hades would take her, so we searched for Morgana. We found her hut in the Desiccated Woods, and she has a new hell hound. He looks young, but when we looked in the window there she was. She was sitting and drinking something out of a goblet, and Morgana was telling her how her family had left her. That if Morgana had not come and rescue her, she would have died. Then we came here to tell you," explained the harpy, then she let out a long breath.

Bella instantly turned on Kahn the words she spoke tore through Kahn's cold heart. "This is all your fault Kahn, if you had never gone after her or put Coda in the Shadow realm this would have never happened," Bella said acidly. Kahn looked at the harpies and barked, "You are dismissed, I will send for you when you are needed."

The harpies scrambled and squawked as they headed for the door. Just before they got to the threshold they heard, "Go and gather your army, and wait for my orders," Bella yelled while never taking her eyes off Kahn. The big oak doors slammed when they closed ringing throughout the castle.

Kahn watched the fire dance in Bella's eyes, the more he watched the more she upset she got. In a room with no windows the wind started to blow causing the picture of Kahn and Bella to crash to the stone floor. Kahn noticed the natural chill that was in the castle was gone. He reached out a hand to lay it on Bella's arm when he saw that she was shaking, and her beautiful green eyes had turned black. Causing him to pull his hand back, and the temperature had risen so high the black and red tapestry hanging on the walls had ignited. Looking around the throne room he saw they were surrounded by flames.

Kahn knew he needed to tell Bella the truth before she killed them both. Thinking quickly, he knew that he needed to get her calm, because she would never listen to him as angry as she was. Closing his eyes, he tried to call the artic winds to put out the fire, when that did not work, he called on Poseidon to help with water. But with Kahn's past Poseidon would not help. Acting on pure nerves Kahn grabbed Bella and crushed his lips to hers. Pushing all the love and calming he had in him to her. Bella's body went stiff, then after what seemed to take forever, she went limp in his arms.

Once Bella collapsed the flames were extinguished. Kahn held Bella in his arms as he sat on the floor in the destruction from Bella's anger. But Kahn knew that this was all his fault for not telling her the truth. Now his family was in real danger because he kept it to himself, instead of trusting his brother or the love of his life with the truth. Kahn watched Bella as she slept. He worked on a plan to help put things right, the way he should have many years ago. In trusting his family and not playing this cat and mouse game with Morgana and thinking he could have taken care of it himself.

Chapter Twenty-Three

In Mount Olympus Zeus sat by Artemis's bedside and called for Apollo. "Son, I need you to do something of great importance. A message needs to get to the third princess, Zanderley. I need you to tell her that the person she is with is not who they seem. That her sisters are coming for her."

"Father, what makes you think I would do this, or that Zanderley would even believe me?" asked Apollo.

Waiving his hand at the bed he said, "Because the young queens saved your sister's life."

Slowly Apollo turned his head and looked at his sister. "What happened to her?" he asked.

"Your sister helped Temprance, Acelyn, and the dragon guardians with a hoard of evil creatures outside of their castle. When your sister got knocked out, they protected her until they got her to safety," explained Zeus.

Without saying another word Apollo nodded then looked at his sister one last time and left to carry out his father's wishes.

Deep in the Desiccated Woods, Zanderley looked around the run-down hut. Every time she got to close to the windows or door, the hell hound would give a warning growl causing her to back away and sit back down at the table. Not knowing if she should trust this person that came to her rescue. Zanderley was looking out the window from her spot at the table when Morgana startled her pulling her out of her thoughts.

"I am going out to grab some supplies, stay here where you are hidden. We do not want Kahn or your evil sisters to find out where you are. Spike will stay here and keep a look out and keep you safe," said Morgana. Then she left, just stopping outside long enough to tell Spike to keep an eye on her and not to let her leave.

Zanderley took this time to move freely around the hut and get a good look at everything. She went over to the wall of jars and studied them.

"Eye of newt, bat wings, dragons' blood, scale of dragon, tongue of snake," she read. "Gross! what does she use this for I wonder." The next place she looked at was the wall of books. Her eyes settled on a dark flesh colored book, reaching out she grabbed it by the spine and held it in her hands. It read Book of Spells, holding the book in one hand she ran the other over the cover. Realizing it was made from flesh she shuttered, she swallowed hard and opened the book. After looking at a few pages she wondered if there was anything in here that would help her escape. Deciding she needed to act quickly she looked through the spells and stopped on one that said sleeping spell.

Looking around quickly for something to write it on she found nothing, so she sucked in a deep breath and ripped the pages she needed out of the book. Zanderley quickly shut the book and put it back on the shelf and folded the papers and stuffed them in the back pocket of her jeans. Then deciding it was not safe to keep them in her pocket she pulled them back out and folded them smaller and stuffed the papers in her bra.

To calm her racing heart, she looked around the hut and started to list how much things were different here than at home. Walking over to the chair she noticed that the seat and the back were covered with a light brown fur pelt, "I wonder if it is from a deer," she thought. Glancing over to the bed she saw that there was a huge fur pelt there as well. Turning to walk over to the bed she heard something outside and not wanting to be caught snooping she made a mad dash back to her spot at the table and sat.

Apollo found Morgana's hut and watched closely to see if there was any movement inside. He watched Morgana stop in the doorway and talk to someone then close the door and talk to the hell hound pup. "Spike, make sure no one disturbs our guest, and do not let her leave, understood? Now that is a good boy," said Morgana then she left. Apollo watched for signs of life in the little hut, while he kept an eye on the pup. Then he saw her, she was just as slender as the other two but just like her sisters her hair was different. She had sun kissed blond hair that was in ringlets that fell past her waist.

Apollo wondered how they all had their hair the same style for not growing up together. Shaking his head bring himself back to the task at hand he watched her as she moved around the hut. Every time she would pass to close to the window the pup would growl. Walking slowly up to the pup Apollo tried the easy way first, but when he started to growl, he hit him with a low wattage lightning bolt, knocking him out. Apollo approached the hut stepping on a stick making it snap, he saw that Zanderley heard him. He watched as she darted back to her seat at the table. At the window he greeted her. "Hello Princess Zanderley, I am Apollo."

With wide eyes her mouth fell open, finding the only words that came out was "The Greek God?"

"Yes, I do not have much time before Morgana comes back. Beware Princess, she is not who she says she is. You cannot trust her; she is an evil sorceress. She is trying to keep you away from your sisters," Apollo explained.

"Are you here to take me to my sisters?"

"No, you must stay here and wait for your sisters to come to you. They will be headed this way once the morning light touches the land."

"What am I going to do about Morgana then? She wants me to kill my sisters and take the throne myself."

"No, if you do that this world will die, you and your sisters must rule together. As for Morgana make her think that you are on her side. You are not strong enough to stand against her on your own, you need your sisters," said Apollo.

"How do I know that I can trust you? Morgana told me that my sisters didn't want me and that they were going to destroy me, because they were working with my evil uncle," asked a very confused Zanderley.

Apollo could feel the change in the air and knew that Morgana was on her way back. He knew that his time with the princess was almost at an end. Acting quickly, he looked at the ground and scooped up a hand full of sand. He waved his other hand over the closed one while speaking softly. Zanderley watched him closely, as she watched she almost fell into a trance like state when she gazed into his eyes. Opening his hand Apollo offered Zanderley the little bottle of shimmering white sand. Reaching a tentative hand out she took the bottle from Apollo.

Studying it closely she asked, "What is this for?"

"That, princess, is magic sand; all you need to do is put a pinch in some water and ask to see your sisters. Then an image of your sisters will appear, then you will know how far or close they are. Make sure that you keep this hidden away from Morgana, if she sees this bottle, she will know that a god has helped you. Now I must go, she is on her way back," explained Apollo.

Zanderley watched as he faded away, then a loud growl made her jump sending her way from the windows. She sat back down at the table looking at the small jar full of sand. "Now where do I hide you?" she thought, while looking around. Remembering the tiny pocket that come in jeans that was normally useless, she tried to fit the bottle in her pocket and was overjoyed when it slipped right in and was undetectable. Just as she sat back down, she heard the latch on the old rickety door. The door squeaked and rubbed the floor whenever it was opened. Once Morgana was in, she looked at Zanderley and smiled. "Now it is time for your first magic lesson."

Chapter Twenty-Four

Zanderley watched as Morgana gathered books and ingredients, then carried them over to the old table where Zanderley was sitting. Looking down Zanderley noticed things looked different after she had her conversation with Apollo. Zanderley was starting to see through the glamour that Morgana had put on everything. The table now had scars and burns that must have come from Morgana's evil mixes going wrong. Zanderley looked around her surrounding once again and this time she saw what was the true reality that surrounded her. The window she had been talking to Apollo out of was broken and would not stay latched shut. The beautiful bed that she had been sleeping on now was just a frame with straw and a matted fur blanket.

Zanderley had to hold back the shudder that wanted to run through her when she looked over at Morgana's altar where she prepped the ingredients for her potions. The back and sides of the altar were covered in black and red candle wax, but what was most disturbing was the worktable part of the altar. It was stained with blood. She knew those stains well, the wonderful woman who raised her is a trauma E.R. nurse. She remembered when her adoptive mom would come home with blood stains on her scrubs. But when Zanderley would get scared from seeing the blood her mom would always let her know that, "Zandy, sweetheart, just because you see the blood doesn't mean that they died." Well, she knew this time that some poor creature had been sacrificed there.

Zanderley was caught up in her own thoughts to make out what Morgana was saying to her, all that she could hear was a small buzzing that sounded far away. Morgana was getting very aggravated because Zanderley was not paying attention to her. So, Morgana picked up the biggest spell book she had and slammed it on the table in front of her causing Zanderley to scream and fall backwards in her chair.

People called Zanderley fearless when she was growing up because nothing really scared her. She always loved watching scary movies, going to haunted house attractions, and ghost hunting with her friends. For the first time in her life, she could honestly say she knew what real fear felt like, looking up at Morgana and without the glamour hiding her identity. The old frail woman was gone, she looked like she was part human and part demon. Morgana had black stringy hair that seemed to have a life of its own. Her eyes glowed red and seemed to pulse, her mouth was full of sharp pointy teeth, and her skin looked like it had dried out in the sun for thousands of years. Her voice hissed, with a demonic tone as she spoke. "Zanderley, you will pay attention when I am trying to teach you."

Zanderley's blood ran cold from fear, all she could do was just stare at the nightmare in front of her. Morgana snarled causing Zanderley to scoot backwards until her back hit the wall which only aggravated Morgana even more, "What is wrong with you, girl? Why are you acting like a scared mouse? Calm down my pretty, princess, I am a friend, I will not hurt you. Remember I saved you when your family left you to rot."

Zanderley remembered what Apollo had told her. "Princess, do not let Morgana know that I have helped you. If she finds out, she will kill you and then go after your sisters. Do not try and be a hero and try and kill her yourself; she is much stronger than you." Taking a deep breath Zanderley shook the fear off. Looking back up at her enemy she gave a shaky smile, "I am sorry, Mistress Morgana, you scared me when you dropped the book. It sent me into a flash back from my childhood. (She lied) When I was little, I was out in the woods and it was hunting season, there was this big, beautiful 12-point buck. I was star struck by his looks; I remember my mom telling me I would get buck fever one of these days. Well, it hit me that day. He was big, and his fur was so black he looked almost blue. I was sitting there watching him when this loud boom sounded and I watched him drop, I ran over to him kneeling next to him, I watched the blood bloom on his side. I stayed there and watched him die. It was an event that scarred my life forever." Zanderley's body relaxed seeing that Morgana was believing the lie.

Morgana's eyes softened and she gave Zanderley an oily smile that showed her sharp teeth. "I am so sorry my dear, I did not mean to scare you," said Morgana as she extended her hand for Zanderley to take.

Zanderley studied Morgana before putting her hand in hers. Morgana's hand was boney with long sharp blackened nails. Zanderley took a deep breath. She placed her hand in Morgana's and stood, she walked back over to the table and sat down. Deciding that she could take advantage of her current situation she picked up a book and asked for Morgana for her guidance.

Chapter Twenty-Five

As the girls ate, they watched their parents. Acelyn was the first to break the silence. "Mother are you sure you and Father can't stay the night?"

"Oh, my sweet darlings, I wish we could stay and help you find your sister, but we cannot. No one can know that we are alive and helping you, if Morgana and Kahn find out they could attack before you girls find your sister. If that happens all will be lost, and we will all perish," explained Anastasia while walking over to Acelyn. Once Anastasia was close enough, Temprance and Acelyn grabbed ahold of her and pulled her close. Anastasia looked down at her daughters, her heart was filled with love and broke for the child that was still lost. She looked up at Alexzander with tears in her eyes and shook her head. Alexzander walked around the large table to join his beloved, running a hand down her back he whispered, "We need to go."

At hearing their father's words Temprance and Acelyn just held on tighter. Anastasia nodded at Alexzander then she laid her cheek on top of her beautiful daughter's head. Knowing that she could stall no longer she moved out of their embrace and told the girls, "There will be time for us all to spend more time as a family once this war is won. I want you girls to be brave, and travel with the speed of the gods. Find your sister and bring her home where she belongs." Leaning in, she kissed Temprance and Acelyn on the forehead then stepped back. Alexzander stepped forward and held his arms out inviting them into his arm. He enveloped them in the warmest hugs that they had ever felt. He kissed each princess on the top of her head and spoke, "Remember you are royalty, each race in Aadya has its own king and queen but you and your sisters will be the queens who will reign over all of Aadya. You bow to no one other than the gods. But remember do not let the power go to your head, you must always be strong, just, and merciful. But only show mercy when it is truly warranted." Then Alexzander released the hold he had on his daughters and once again joined Anastasia he draped an arm around her waist and smiling one last time then they disappeared.

Anton and Zeke watched as their mates just stood there in silence, they could feel a storm of emotions that were coiling in them. They looked at each other and knew they needed to try and defuse the ticking time bombs that the girls held inside. Saying nothing they walked up to their mates and enfolded them in their embrace. Speaking softly Zeke spoke to Temprance. "Come, My Love, sit with me a while." Zeke led her over to one of the great thrones in the room and sat pulling her onto his lap. Anton followed suit but once Anton sat down, Acelyn pulled out of his embrace. Acelyn let out a scream that echoed throughout the castle. She was not able to hold the storm inside any longer, she ran over to the table still full of food from dinner and screamed again.

Feeling helpless Anton walked over to her and tried to comfort her. Spinning around she placed both hands on his chest and pushed. "Stop! I don't want to be held!" Turning and facing the table once more she screamed, the change was on her before she could stop it. Looking down at his love, he knew that he needed to treat her with kid gloves because with her in tiger form, she was deadly. Acelyn stalked towards Anton, not knowing what she was going to do, he walked backwards keeping his eyes on her.

Anton did not notice that Jaz and Jewel had taken off and were now behind one of the thrones for safety. Looking out from behind the throne, Jewel spoke loud enough that Anton could hear her. "Anton, be careful with the mood she is in, she is completely unpredictable," warned Jewel.

With a nod, he took note of his surroundings and realized that the room was big enough to shift. Backing away faster he moved far enough away so that he could shift without hurting anyone. Anton let the shift take hold, his neck lengthened. His face took shape and horns grew from his skull. His arms and legs grew to mammoth size and claws pushed out where his fingernails were that scored the marble floor. His tail was as long as his body was. His tan skin had turned into silver scales with his underbelly and inside of his wings black.

Even in candlelight he seemed to sparkle and shine like gems. With him in his shifted form he could feel all the emotions that his beloved was holding inside of her. Anton took a deep breath in and when he let it out, he snorted silver puffs of smoke.

Temprance watched her sister with trepidation because she did not know what her sister would do. Zeke held Temprance just a little tighter when he started feeling her muscles start to ripple. Leaning forward Zeke whispered in Temprance's ear, "Do not interfere. This is for them to work out. Remember Anton loves her very much, he will not hurt your sister, and Acelyn loves Anton. They will be fine; Anton is the only one that can calm her down without being hurt," said Zeke bending his neck so he could kiss Temprance in the crook of her neck.

"Zeke, my sister would never hurt me intentionally, how can he help her, and I can't?" Temprance whispered.

"Do you remember when we are in our shifted forms, we can feel each other's emotions?" he asked.

While never taking her eyes off her sister she nodded.

"Well, it is the same for them. He can feel what is going on inside of her. Also, you are right my dear, Acelyn would never hurt you intentionally, but with her like this she is unpredictable. She is acting on her emotions only, Acelyn is not thinking with a clear head," Zeke explained.

So Temprance watched her sister while her heart ached. Acelyn felt like she was going to explode, she felt herself spiraling out of control and there was nothing she could do to stop it. Acelyn could hear a voice trying to break through her thoughts, but the pain from her emotions was just too strong. All she wanted to do was to make it stop.

Anton did not know for sure if he was breaking through in her thoughts. So, he watched her body and knew when she was about to pounce. Anton watched Acelyn's muscles quiver and shake, just before she pounced, he saw her muscles bunch for the jump.

Acelyn landed, sinking her teeth and claws in the soft part of Anton's neck just above his chest. Letting out a deep roar from the pain, Anton turned his head and grabbed Acelyn by the scruff of her neck. When he ripped her off, he felt his flesh tearing and his blood ran like rivers down his chest pooling on the marble floor. Shaking her hard enough to disorientate her, he then tossed her a few feet away hoping that did the trick.

Climbing back up on all fours, Acelyn shook her head and started to stalk back towards Anton. Temprance could not watch anymore, pulling out of Zeke's arms she ran and stood in front of her sister. Praying that Acelyn would not look right through her, Temprance stood her ground between Acelyn and Anton.

"ACELYN! stop this nonsense, pull yourself together. Look at what you did to Anton, you need to stop before you do something you will never forgive yourself for," Temprance said calmly. But Acelyn heard nothing, the only thing that was going through her head was release. The more she raged the better she felt. Acelyn crouched low and jumped. Temprance covered her face and sucked in her breath and held it waiting on the impact. When she heard her sister snarling and growling, she turned and watched the horror unfold in front of her.

Anton knew once he saw Princess Temprance stand in between Acelyn and him she was in danger. So, he taunted his beloved to come after him. Once he knew she took the bait and jumped, he incased his body with his wings. When Acelyn landed she bit and ripped the webbing of his wings with her claws. By the time Acelyn started to tire out she could not hold the tiger form any longer. When her form faded away, Acelyn was covered in blood and beating her fist against his torn and battered wings. Anton let his dragon form fade away once she started crying. Saying nothing he bent down and picked her up cradling her in his arms. Anton looked over at Temprance and said, "I am going to take her so she can get cleaned up. We will be back. Do not worry Princess, I will take care of her." Then he just turned and walked out of the throne room.

In what must have been the king's and queen's chamber he sat her down next to the stone pool. Speaking softly, he asked her, "Dove, may I see your hand?" Saying nothing she lifted her hand to him. Anton gripped her hand softly then he placed it on the side of the pool. The stone shook and turned to dust, leaning down he kissed her on her bloody forehead and said, "Stay here Dove, I will be right back." Anton stood and with one last look at Acelyn he left the room.

Chapter Twenty-Six

Anton moved quickly through the castle, every step he took echoed throughout the stone halls. Anton's thoughts raced through his mind. He was very worried about his beloved Acelyn and how this event would affect her. Shaking his head to clear his thoughts he searched his memories from when he was younger, trying to remember where the sparkling pool was at in the castle. Quickly turning left and heading down the stairs out of the castle to the arches that held the most beautiful roses. He remembered running under them with Zeke, Coda, and Malic when they were kids, and how the sun peaked through the leaves and vines. Now it was all stone, no colors, and it was dark as a tunnel, knowing he needed to hurry he ran praying that the pool was left untouched because of its magic.

Once Anton could see the pool, he let out a sigh of relief when he saw that the water shined and glistened in the moon light. The air shimmered around his hand when he reached down for the bucket. Anton reached down and picked up one of the buckets laying on the side of the pool, and the air shimmered around him. Looking up the sight he saw punched the air out of his chest. Aadya was beautiful once again, the sparkling pool had protected itself from the curse. Making a vow to bring the princesses here in the morning, he said a thank you to the gods and filled the bucket with water. Once he stepped back the air shimmered and Aadya was dark and gray once again. Moving quickly without spilling the water in the bucket he hurried back to Acelyn.

In the throne room the rest of the heroes cleaned up the mess. Turning and looking a Zeke, Temprance asked, "I just don't understand why did she jump over me? It was like she didn't even see me there."

"Temprance my love, please do not take offense to that. Your sister was too far gone in animalistic rage for you to get through to her. She had her sights set on Anton; it was also good that she targeted him. If she would have targeted you, she would have killed you. It would not have been on purpose, and even if she did not kill you, you would have been gravely injured." Walking over to her he gently lifted her head so he could look into her beautiful eyes. "You know that your sister would never forgive herself if she hurt you."

Two tears escaped when she nodded in agreement with Zeke. Temprance let out a shuddering breath trying to calm herself before speaking. "But she hurt Anton badly."

"I know Agape Mu, but he heals quickly, he is a dragon, he will be fine" said Zeke.

Reaching up she wrapped her arms around his neck and Zeke knew when she laid her head on his chest her beautiful violet eyes still shined from tears. Quietly Jaz, Jewel, and Coda finished cleaning up. While Coda helped the others clean, he tried to ignore the sadness in his heart from knowing that his mate was still in the clutches of Morgana.

When Anton made it back to Acelyn his heart broke even more seeing the love of his life laying there on the floor, her hair was matted, clothes torn, and her body covered in blood, he also noticed her body shaking from her weeping. Anton sat the bucket of water down next to the stone bathing pool and bent down to pick up Acelyn. When she noticed his touch, she tried to recoil from him, remembering the damage she had done. He spoke to her in a soft but firm voice, "Dove, do not push me away, let me help you." Acelyn kept her head bowed while she shook her head no. Not taking no for an answer he sat down and pulled her onto his lap. Once seated there, he wrapped his arms around her and focused to make their breathing in sync. Anton could feel Acelyn start to calm down, so he spoke softly once again. "Dove, come let me help you get cleaned up." Acelyn just shook her head. "Acelyn, baby, please no more tears it rips out my heart every time I see you cry," stated Anton.

Acelyn looked up at the man she loved with a blood and tear stained face. Swallowing hard she finally croaked out, "How can you look at me after what I did to you?"

"Because my Dove, you are my mate the other half of my soul. I wanted you to go after me," he said with a soft smile.

She pulled away from Anton so she could look in his eyes, "Why would you want me to attack you?"

Raising a hand, he cupped her cheek, "Because if you would have targeted anyone else you would have killed them. I knew if you would have killed anyone, it would have destroyed you. With you attacking me I knew you would not. So, you see with us being bound we cannot fight to the death. Our souls would never allow it to happen," explained Anton.

Sensing that she was finally calm he loosened his arms, pulling away she slowly got to her feet and looked around and asked, "Anton, where are we?"

"We are in the Queen's bathing chamber." Holding out a hand for her to take, "Come let us get you fixed and cleaned up," said Anton.

Looking down at his hand she laid her hand in his. He gave her hand a little tug until she was standing next to him. Letting go of her hand he bent down and picked up the bucket and dumped the water in the stone and marble bathing pool. Acelyn noticed that the water shined and sparkled. Looking up at his beautiful mate he explained, "Okay Dove, all you need to do is put your hand in the water and tell it what scent you would like, and it will be done."

Looking at him like he was crazy she bent at the waist and placed her hand in the water and said, "Lavender." The air shimmered and then the room was filled with the scent of lavender, and the bathing pool water now had small purple flowers floating in the water. Acelyn jumped back and looked at Anton, with a small smile she bent and put her hand back in the water and said warm. Steam rose from the pool and Acelyn looked back up at Anton and smiled. Standing up she started to remove her clothes, looking over at Anton she asked, "Will you join me?"

Anton just watched her to make sure she was okay and not trying to suppress her feelings again. Once he was satisfied, he nodded and started to remove his clothes. When he pulled off his shirt Acelyn reached out a tentative hand to the gashes that was scored across his chest. She looked up at him with tears shining in her eyes. She laid the palm of her hand in between the gashes and before she could speak he shook his head. "They will heal my love, as will the bite mark on my neck. Do not cry I will be fine, and do not let this weigh on you. If you do it will cloud your mind and you will not be able to do what is needed," Anton said softly.

Gripping her hand softly he lifted it from his chest and helped her into the pool. After she was seated, he finished undressing and joined her in the pool sitting across from her. Knowing she could do one more thing to help him, she cupped some water in her hand and closed her eyes wishing for the water to heal. Rising to her knees she let the water flow out of her hands onto the wounds on Anton and watched them, the gashes closed to where they were only deep red lines were left. Getting ready to repeat the process, Anton stopped her.

"You have done enough they will heal the rest of the way. By morning there will be no trace of them left, I am a dragon, we heal much faster than humans. Now let me take care of you." He reached out and grabbed her and made her squeal when he pulled her to him and spun her around, so she was nestled between his legs. He reached over the edge and grabbed the bucket and filled it with water then slowly he dumped it over her head. Anton repeated this process until Acelyn was clean and begged him to stop. She reached back and grabbed the bucket and put it over the edge. She scooted back so her back met his front and she snuggled in. Grabbing his arms, she wrapped them around her, and she finally let out a long breath and let the lavender work.

After what seemed like hours they climbed out of the pool and surprised when she was out, she was dry? "Umm, Anton how are we dry, we just got out of the water?" asked Acelyn.

Anton handed her the pack that had extra clothes as he answered, "The water that we bathed in was from a special pool that is magical. I do not know how it works but the one thing I do know is that only the royal family can use it. If someone outside of the royal family tries to use it, it will only be water," explained Anton.

Feeling just a little exposed and bone tired, Acelyn dressed quickly. While waiting on Anton to finish getting dressed, she looked around what would have been her parents bathing room. Her eyes settled on a small divan with what looked like cloth draped over the arm. Acelyn walked over to it, bending at the waist she slowly ran her hand over the seat of the divan to the cloth. Anton watched in amazement as the stone fell away and the colors that were trapped came to life once again. From the angle Anton was at he could see the wonderment fill Acelyn's eyes when she reached down and caressed the soft black fur. Walking up behind Acelyn he slid an arm around her waist to rest his hand on her stomach.

Looking down over her shoulder he turned his head to nuzzle her ear and asked, "What is going on in that beautiful head of yours?"

As she extended her fingers so the palm of her hand laid flat on the fur as she spoke. "Anton this is my mother's, I wonder how many nights she sat here getting ready for bed and she dreamed of us? Just look at the pattern in the fur. You would think she had it dyed for us."

"What do you mean? What makes you think that?" asked Anton.

Moving her hand, she said, "Look at the flowers, the red rose would be for Temprance, white rose for Zanderley, and the black and white rose for me. But I don't know what this one would be for?" said Acelyn resting her hand on the vine of purple morning glories.

"If she had the flowers for her children, that would mean the purple flowers are for Malic, your brother," said Anton softly.

Acelyn pulled her hand back as if she had been burned. "Oh, that never crossed my mind," she said sadly. Anton broke the silence and said, "Come Dove, let us go back and join the others before your sister thinks I ran off with you."

Turning her head, she looked up at him and smiled. Releasing the hold, he had on her Anton stepped back and picked up their packs, holding out his hand he waited for Acelyn. She slipped her hand into his and they walked together in silence back to the throne room.

Chapter Twenty-Seven

Malic knew he could no longer sit on the sidelines when the rules have already been broken by Morgana. Hoping that his actions would not impact what his sisters needed to do he summoned Hades.

Hail to the Gods hear my plea,
I summon lord of the underworld,
Hades come to me and hear my plea,
so that I may help my sisters with their destiny,
So, mote it me.

I did not take long before there was a loud popping sound and a portal of fire appeared and the Lord of the Underworld walked through. Malic spread his winds and bowed his head and waited for Hades to address him.

What seemed like hours later Malic felt the heat and electricity of magic in the air when Hades moved closer to him. Worried he would be punished he almost cringed when Hades placed his hand on top of Malic's head and gave him a soft stroke.

In a soft but accented voice Hades spoke, "Tell me young prince, why have you summoned me?"

Malic had always been fascinated how Hades had a different accent to his voice than the other Gods. Taking a chance, he turned his head so he could seek a peek at the Lord of the Underworld. Malic was caught off guard when he saw that the Lord of the Underworld had a smirk on his flawless face.

Once again Hades spoke, "Look at me young prince, and answer me. There must be an exceptionally good reason you have summoned me here."

Not wanting Hades to become inpatient, Malic tucked in his wings and stood tall getting his first good look at the God. He had long black hair and his eyes were a dark purple almost black instead of white glowing orbs. He was in his battle armor, black leather pants, his boots came up past his calves, his shirt was a mixture between leather and dark purple tunic. In his left hand he carried a spear. There had been some rumors that it was the spear of destiny, but no one could be sure because, no one had ever laid eyes on it before.

"My Lord Hades, I am sorry to summon you, and I know I am not allowed to interfere with what my sisters are doing but they need help. Morgana has cheated and broke the rules," said Malic with a slight tremble in his voice.

Hades studied the brave little prince and let what he said sink in. Then he asked, "What is that you are speaking of?"

Swallowing past the lump in his throat, Malic spoke more confident, "Morgana has changed the rules and has changed my sisters' destiny. Morgana has kidnaped my sister Zanderley. Plus, Morgana has taken another one of your pups."

Malic felt the air change, electricity sparked and popped. Malic studied the change in Hades eyes they were now blue dancing flames. Looking down on his gate keeper Hades tried to reign in his anger to assess what he was just told. "Explain, Little Prince. What do you mean by all of this?"

Malic shook his head and started at the beginning telling Hates everything, from Coda going to the shadow realm and Zanderley being taken by Kahn, to the girls getting only a part of their powers and Morgana going to the underworld and stealing a Cerberus pup. "You see my sisters are all in Aadya now and the curse is half broken. The big problem is that Morgana has my sister Zanderley and the other two fought in a big battle with Artemis and saved her life. Temprance and Acelyn are leaving once the morning light touches the land to go rescue Zanderley. I am just afraid they will fail because things have been changed and the Fates are still in stone," said Malic finally coming to the end of the story and feeling tired.

Hades started to pace back and forth thinking how he could help without messing with the balance very much. Hades turned and looked at Malic. "Little

Prince, I think I can help your sisters without upsetting the balance too much. I will go and retrieve my pup. I will make it look like my pup escaped during the night. That will leave Morgana scrambling and distracted on finding him so that your sisters can get close."

Malic almost wept with relief, he looked up at Hades with a lonely tear sliding down his feathered cheek. "Thank you, Lord Hades, for the help you are doing."

"No need for tears Little Prince, we all just want what is best for Aadya," said Hades with just a little hint in his voice that left Malic thinking that he was going to enjoy this a little too much.

Just as Hades turned to leave Malic spoke up, "Lord Hades, my I ask you one more question?" asked Malic.

Hades stopped and asked, "What is your question, Little Prince?"

"Why do you call me that?" Malic asked softly.

Hades turned and walked back to the black phoenix and gave him a soft stroke down his back. "Because no matter what happened to you or what form you are in now, you will always be a Prince. Take pride in that do not ever think that you are less of a Prince just because your life was cut way too short. No one can ever take that title away from you. You are doing Aadya a great service by helping your sisters, and soon you will be reunited with your parents if I have any say in the matter." With one last stroke down Malic's back Hades turned. With a loud pop the flaming portal opened, and he was gone. Malic sat in the silence and thought about what Hades had said.

Hades walked through the Underworld to his palace calling out for Persephone. "Where are you, My Beloved Wife?

"I am here, Husband, what is with all the yelling, what is wrong?" asked Persephone walking up to Hades placing her hands on his chest.

Hades watched his beautiful wife walk towards him. She was breathtaking, Persephone had the sides of her long chestnut brown hair braided and wrapped around her head and shaped into a crown. The back side of her hair was so long it brushed her heels when she walked. Her dress was held up with a knot on her right shoulder and was a sheer dark teal that went to her feet in the front, and a long train followed her in the back. The dress was accented with a white leather band that rested just under the globes of her breasts, and on the front of the dress there were two slits, one on each leg that went from foot to hip. So, when she walked you could see her leather sandals that laced just below the knees.

"Did you know one of the pups was taken, my dear?" Hades asked her.

With a look of surprise, she answered, "No, who would be foolish enough to come down here and take one of the pups?"

Pulling away so that his anger did not hurt his beloved, he turned and walked away while yelling angrily, "Morgana!"

"Morgana?" Persephone said in surprise while lifting her hand to her mouth. "But how did she make it in here without Despair knowing?" she asked looking down at the sleeping Cerberus.

"I do not know but that will be one thing I find out, also she has the third sister in her clutches. Morgana is trying to get Zanderley to use magic to kill Temprance and Acelyn. I must be thankful that my nephew came to see her and let her know that her sisters are coming to rescue her not to lose hope," explained Hades

Walking back over to Hades, Persephone placed her hands on his back sliding them around so she could rest them on his chest. Hugging him tightly she laid her cheek on his back and asked, "What are your plans now, Dear Husband?"

Turning in her arms he lifted her face to meet his and with a soft kiss he said, "I am going to go get my pup back and see if I can put a snag in Morgana's plans. Because none of us will know what is going to happen until the others wake up the Sisters of Fate." With one last kiss he tuned and disappeared.

Hades walked in the dead of night towards Morgana's hut in the Desiccated Woods. Hades sniffed the air and knew he was close, "I smell brimstone." Hades walked so light he left no sound in his wake, as he walked, he took in his surroundings. "I wonder why this place was untouched by the curse," he thought. As Hades crept closer to the hut the smell of brimstone only grew stronger. Once the hut was in sight, he had to calm his breathing and his thoughts, because he knew if he messed this up all would be lost. He needed to get to the pup and get back to the Underworld without being seen.

Hades was now close enough to see his pup sleeping soundly in the moonlight. Reaching in his pouch that was hung from his belt, he took out a bloody piece of meat he used to train his pups. Giving a soft whistle that rode on the wind, the pup lifted its heads. Letting out a whimper, he looked at Hades then laid his head back down. Confused he walked up a little closer and called out to him, "Come here, Death." The pup only lifted its heads and whimpered and laid back down. But this time Hades saw the red ruby glow on his collar. "Oh, Bloody Hell!" Walking over to the pup he crouched down and inspected his collar. "Let me see if I can remove this," he said while stroking the pup sending him into ecstasy. Running his hands around the collar he noticed there was no way to unhook it, "Damn, it must be enchanted" he thought. Knowing he just could not remove it without hurting the pup he thought in silence, and that is when he heard it.

Zanderley watched as the drop-dead gorgeous man walked towards the hut. Once he was close enough, she fought to keep her gasp quiet when she noticed that he was not just any man but a God. She crouched and crept quietly over to the window so she could watch the God to see what he was doing. She watched as he tried to call the pup over to him. When that failed, the God came closer ducking below the windowsill hoping he would not see her. She listened to the God talk to the pup, but when it got quiet, she took a chance to look and see if he was gone. Zanderley quickly found out that it was the wrong thing to do. Once she could see out the window, she saw nothing so leaning out the window she looked down at where the pup lay and met orbs of blue fire.

Hades quickly put a finger to his lip telling her to hush and not make a sound to wake Morgana. Standing, he reached in the window and plucked her up like she was just a doll. Sitting her down on the ground he waived his hand and the air shimmered making a soundless barrier around them. Zanderley just stood and looked up at him with her mouth hanging open.

With a light smirk on his lips, he asked "Well Young Queen, is that any way to greet a God?

Zanderley knew that she needed to say something but all that would come out was a small squeak. Shaking her head, she gathered her thoughts and tried again. Bowing she apologized, "I am so sorry for the disrespect, but I don't even know your name."

With a small chuckle he bent down so he was eye level with her and said, "My name is Hades, and this is Death," he said pointing down at the pup.

Zanderley took a step back knowing that she was standing in front of the Lord of the Underworld. Reaching out quickly to stop her from moving out of the sound barrier, he spoke softly so he would not spook her any further, "Shh, calm down Princess, I will not hurt you. I am here to help you, but it looks like I am needing your help."

Reaching out she touched his arm to make sure that she was not hallucinating. Feeling more confident that she was not crazy she took two steps forward. Then asked, "What can I do to help you?"

Reaching down, Hades pointed at the collar around Death's neck, "This collar is preventing him from following my commands. I need to remove it so I can take him home, Morgana stole him away from his litter mates."

Tilting her head to one side thinking Zanderley asked, "What can I do?"

"Well Princess, you and your sisters are incredibly special not only can you shift into your tiger form you can cast magic as well. I just might have a chance to overpower Morgana's enchantment with your touch," said Hades.

Shaking her head, "I cannot get anywhere near him she has ordered him to attack me if I get to close."

"I promise you Princess, that Death will not harm you. He is the sweetest out of the litter of pups." Leaning down he laid his hand on top of one of its heads and explained. "Death, the Princess is going to help you out of that collar, do not harm her, do you understand me?" Hades asked. Death looked at his master with loyalty and love in its eyes and nodded its middle head. Hades looked up at Zanderley and nodded at her.

With a cautious hand, she stoked Death on the head and bent down. Running her hand down his neck to the collar. With her other hand she ran her hand around the other side of the collar trying to find the clasp, but she could not find one. Dropping her hands, she studied the collar. Reaching up she touched the ruby in the front. She let out a small gasp when the air around the collar shimmered and turned into an old vine, when she grabbed the vine it turned into dust leaving Death's neck bare. Letting out an excited squeak she looked up at Hades and said, "Oh my, I did not think that was going to work."

Stroking his pup, he looked up at the Princess and smiled, "Thank you, I want to let you know you and your sisters are going to make wonderful queens. This is just what Aadya needs, I would love to sit and talk to you more but the longer we take comes closer to Morgana catching us," explained Hades. In one swift move he stood picking her back up and placing her back in the hut. Lifting her hand, he kissed it. "Princess, your sisters are coming for you. Stay here, and do not let on what happened here tonight."

Zanderley watched as Hades walked away with Death. Smiling to herself knowing she did something of good. Then she watched in amazement when a portal of fire opened and Hades and Death walked through, and they were gone. Sneaking back to her bed, she made sure not to make a sound. Once covered up with the fur, she wished for morning and her sisters.

Chapter Twenty-Eight

As soon as Temprance saw Acelyn and Anton enter the throne room, she jumped up from where she was cuddling with Zeke and ran to her sister. The others joined soon after. Once Temprance reached Acelyn she looked her over to make sure she was okay, nodding in satisfaction she finally spoke, "Ace, are you okay really?"

Not being able to hold back any further she gripped her sister in a fierce hug and cried the last of her frustration out. Softly Acelyn wept saying, "I hurt Anton really bad, how can he still love me after that?"

Temprance looked at her sister and smiled while wiping a tear that slid down her cheek and said, "Acelyn, when you find love like we have it just doesn't go away. The kind of love that you and Anton have is the love that lasts for an eternity. Don't ever doubt that, now come on we need to get some sleep so we can go after our sister."

Walking over to the rest of the gang, Acelyn looked over at her sister and asked, "Hey Tempie, I thought you wanted to explore the castle?"

"Well, I did but now it just doesn't seem right to go exploring without Zanderley," stated Temprance.

Acelyn sat down on the bed made from pillows and furs that Anton had prepared. She watched her sister in complete bliss snuggling down with Zeke. Acelyn looked around the throne room checking on her family then laid her head down on Anton's shoulder and closed her eyes. The last thought before sleep took her, was that her family was almost complete.

As her sisters slept, Zanderley lie awake counting the minutes until day-break. When the moon was high in the night sky her eye lids were too heavy to stay open. As soon as her eyes shut, the nightmare took hold.

Zanderley found herself walking through a beautiful forest, she was enchanted with the soft songs and dancing lights in the trees. Bending down to pick a beautiful dark purple flower, she was startled when the voice seemed to come out of the air. "I would not touch that if I were you." Pulling her hand back she looked around trying to find out where it came from and asked, "Why is it so beautiful? Is this your forest?" The laugh that came made her feel uneasy. "Ha ha, no pretty princess, that is deadly nightshade. It may be exceptionally beautiful, but it is deadly. We would not want anything to happen to you, now do we?" said the voice in the wind.

Feeling unsafe, Zanderley slowly stood and walked to the dirt path. Looking around one more time to try and find where the voice was coming from, she spoke, "Well it has been fun, but I need to go now." Turning quickly, she started walking hoping she picked the right way that would lead her out of the forest. No matter how fast or far she walked the voice on the wind followed her. "Well pretty princess, you are all alone. This is not a safe place, there are many dangers here. There are hungry creatures that have not eaten in a long time that are looking for a meal. You, my dear, would make a great meal."

Zanderley stopped and looked at her surroundings and noticed that the dancing lights were gone and so were the songs. Placing a fist over her heart to try and calm it down because it felt like it was trying to beat out of her chest. She found the courage and yelled back, "I'm not alone. I have sisters and we are looking for each other. I will find them."

In a pitting voice the wind spoke, "Oh, you poor thing did you not know they are hunting you, not saving you. They find you weak and not worthy to rule next to them. Why do you think that your dragon guardian never made it to you? Or why your sisters have not come for you yet? Think about it, princess, you are being hunted and soon you will be dead just like your little brother and your parents. Now I can help you stay alive so you can reign over Aadya. All you need to do is kill your sisters before they can get to you. Now what do you say, are you willing to take my help, so you survive? Or will you die? It is your choice, princess?"

Lifting her head, she looked to the treetops and anger flashed in her eyes. "NO! I do not want your help. You are trying to fill my head with lies. I will find my sisters and we will prove you wrong." Zanderley started running, hoping she would find the exit to the woods soon. But the longer she ran the darker it got. Looking around she noticed her beautiful forest had turned dull and dark. It looked like the life and color had been sucked out of the trees and her footsteps sounded hollow that echoed. Wishing for her sisters she slowed down to a brisk walk. "Temprance, Acelyn, where are you?" Zanderley sniffled. Feeling a chill in the air she rubbed her arms to warm them, and that is when she heard the deep growls. Looking behind her, she noticed that there were two massive tigers. The tigers stalked towards her, when they were close enough, they circled her making her feel as if she was their prey. Watching them closely Zanderley started to move towards the edge of the circle. When she would move too close one would growl and swipe at her with claws. Zanderley moved back to the center and tried to talk to them.

"Temprance, Acelyn, it's me Zanderley, your sister." The burgundy and white tiger stopped and tipped her head to the side studying her. Zanderley walked closer to Temprance and noticed that she must be under a spell because her violet eyes were clouded over. Zanderley knew if she did not break the spell that was over her sisters she would die. Hoping that Temprance would not attack she walked over and reached out to place her hand on Temprance's neck. When she was close enough, she whispered the same words Apollo whispered to her to break Morgana's spell:

Hail to the gods hear my plea,
Let the princess really see,
Clear her mind and vision
So that she can see her destiny
So, mote it be.

The tigers howled and yelled shaking their heads, then their form faded and there were her sisters. As soon as they stood up to great Zanderley the world went black. When Zanderley got her vision back she was in a deep pit and the voice on the wind was back. "I told you that you will never reunite with your sisters. You will do things my way or you will die."

Zanderley woke with her heart pounding, she turned her head to the left and let out a blood curdling scream. Jumping out of her bed, she ran for the door in Morgana's hut. She was almost out the door when she felt searing pain in her neck from her choker. Looking back at Morgana, Zanderley cried, "Please let me go."

Morgana twisted a strand of her oily hair in her fingers and smiled wide, showing her demon sharp teeth. When she spoke, a chill settled over Zanderley, the voice matched the one in her nightmare. "No pretty princess, you will do my bidding and if you do not your sisters will die."

Remembering what Apollo said, Zanderley lowered her head in defeat and said, "What do you need me to do?" Morgana smiled knowing she had won. She held out a hand for Zanderley to take. "Come my dear, it is time for your magic lesson."

Zanderley put her hand in Morgana's making a silent vow that they would kill this sadistic bitch if it were the last thing they did.

Chapter Twenty-Nine

Just before the sun kissed the land Anton woke Acelyn with a soft kiss. A slow smile spread across Acelyn's face, and with a little body wiggle she snuggled back down in the soft pillow bed. Leaning in, he nuzzled her neck, "Dove, come with me. I would like to show you something so beautiful it will take your breath away."

Acelyn's eyes fluttered open, "I doubt anything could be better than this," said Acelyn snuggling in tighter to Anton. Sitting up Anton pulled Acelyn to sit up as well, seeing she was about to protest he put a finger to her lips, "SHHH." Anton could tell she was going to lie back down, so he stood and pulled her to her feet. They walked over to the double doors to the throne room and praying that the doors made no sound, he eased one of the doors open just enough for them to slip through.

Anton looked over to Acelyn and smiled, "We need to hurry, or we will miss it." Taking her hand, he gave it a tiny tug before they started running down the hall to the east watch tower. When they reached the door at the top Acelyn placed her hand on the door making the stone crumble and fall away. Pushing the door open they walked out into the dark morning. Looking around Acelyn saw nothing spectacular, she focused on the moon taking a mental note on the differences between the moons in both realms. "In Edan the moon has a blue tint and the craters in the moon cast shadows that form a face. The one here in Aadya is pure white and looks like a fortune teller's crystal ball." Acelyn turned her head and watched as Anton's human form faded.

Walking over to her he lowered his wing and spoke, "Come here Dove, and climb up."

Placing her hand on the base of his neck she stepped in the crook of his wing, and Acelyn climbed up and seated herself in the saddle on his back. Anton stretched out his wings and took flight. Acelyn watched as the castle got smaller and the ground was no longer in sight. When Anton was high enough, he hovered and spoke, "Watch the horizon, Dove."

"Anton, what am I looking for? It is so dark the only light I see is the moon."

"Patience Dove, it will be here any minute."

Just as Acelyn was about to speak, the sun started to rise. The sight before her made her breath catch and tears started to fall. The morning sky was filled with beautiful colors. Anton could feel that her heart was filled with love and wonder but he was confused to why she was crying. "Acelyn, My Dove, why all the tears? I hoped this would make you happy."

Anton hung his head in defeat and started to descend so he could land. Acelyn spoke, "No, My Love, please can we stay just a little longer it is so beautiful." Turning his head, he looked back at her. She had one hand over her heart, tears running down her face, and the most beautiful smile Anton had ever seen. Nodding he flew back up so she could finish watching the sunrise over her kingdom.

The bright burst of colors seemed to blend into each other. It reminded Acelyn of looking through a prism. The dark pink was the closest to the ground then faded into orange, and the orange transformed to the brightest yellow that Acelyn had ever seen. She studied her kingdom when the sun touched the land, and she thought, "Wow all of this will be mine and my sisters. Oh, I pray to the Gods we have the strength and the courage to defeat our enemy and take back our kingdom." Anton's voice broke through her thoughts, "Dove, we need to get back to the others." Reaching down she stroked his neck and said, "Thank you, after yesterday I needed this. I am ready to face the day and find my sister." Letting out a puff of silver smoke Anton nodded and started back to the castle. When they landed Acelyn slid off and waited for him to shift and when she knew he was sturdy she jumped him. She wrapped her arms around his neck, Anton put an arm under her bottom and nudged her causing her legs to wrap around his waist.

Speaking softly, she spoke, "How did you know that I needed to see that? It still scares me that you know what my needs and wants are, and you know how I am feeling. I am not used to having anyone there for me. My stepmom cared about me, but she was always working. I do not want to sound like a broken record, but thank you again."

Hugging her even tighter Anton spoke from his heart. "Dove, you will always have me by your side. I love you! You are my Queen, lover, and warrior princess. I will always make sure your needs are taken care of. Now let us go join the others then we will go and save your sister."

Anton and Acelyn just nicely got back to the throne room when the others started to stir. Temprance was the first to open her eyes. She smiled at Acelyn then she closed her eyes and snuggled back down with Zeke. Looking around the room Acelyn watched as her family started to wake. Her stomach growled so loud it echoed causing Zeke to speak up. "I really hope that was for hunger." With her eyes still closed Temprance slapped Zeke's chest causing him to wince and rub the stinging flesh.

Sniffing the air Acelyn spoke, "Please tell me that smell is for real food and not me going crazy from hunger?" Anton spoke as he turned her around to face the table, "Look Dove, someone was thinking of you ladies this morning." When Acelyn saw the table full of food she walked over to it and read the note.

Good morning my babies,

Make sure you eat a good breakfast, the obstacles that still stand in front of you will be difficult. But your father and I have faith in you. Remember to pack food for your travels, and good luck. May you travel with the speed of the Gods and be careful.

One more thing, I love you, my babies.

With never ending love,

Mother and Father

Holding the note to her chest she called to Temprance, "Sis, all this is from Mom and Dad, they even sent a note."

"Please, for the love of the Gods is there coffee?" asked Temprance causing everyone to laugh.

"Yes, dear sister, I see there is coffee along with, fresh fruit, pancakes, eggs, ham, bacon, even rounds of bread."

Jumping to her feet she raced to the table, "Wait. What pancakes? How do we have pancakes?" Walking to the table scratching his head Coda asked, "What is pancakes?"

Putting three pancakes on a plate and drowning them in butter and syrup with a grin Temprance said, "These are pancakes and they smell divine."

Shaking his head Coda commented, "Those are breakfast sweet bread, not pancakes, silly princess." Seeing then that her sister was about to argue to defend her favorite breakfast Acelyn spoke up. "Coda, where we are from, they are called pancakes. So, before you two get in another debate on names of things, just know that you both are talking about the same thing. They just have two different names in each realm. Now we all need to sit down and eat before my sister gets bitchy because she is hungry and has not had any coffee."

Getting ready to scold her sister she looked over at her and busted up laughing seeing the shit-eating grin on Acelyn's face. Acelyn watched the dynamic between each couple. Zeke and Temprance leaned towards each other and talked quietly while they filled their plates. Acelyn just shook her head thinking to herself, "How in the world does my sister eat so much but not gain a pound?" Jaz and Jewel ate in silence, and every time Jewel reached for something Jaz was just a little quicker and placed it on her plate. She could see the sorrow just hanging around Coda. Acelyn knew how he felt, left out and all alone even though there are people around you. Leaning over to Anton she kissed his cheek and said, "I will be right back."

Acelyn stood causing everyone to stop eating and watch her. She walked around the table and stood behind Coda. Taking a deep breath, she hugged him and spoke softly, "Do not worry Coda, we will find her. As soon as we are done eating, we will leave." After placing a kiss to the top of his head she walked back to her seat and began to eat. Picking up a strawberry and placing the ripe fruit between her lips she moaned when she bit down. The strawberry had the perfect flavor just the right amount of tart and sweet. When she opened her eyes, she noticed everyone was still watching her. She cast her eyes down and her cheeks went pink, to get the attention off her, she lifted her hand and motioned that everyone should continue.

While her sisters finished up eating and packed their bags, Zanderley sat on her bed thinking of a way to escape and trying not to wake Morgana. "How am I going to get out of this? I need to do something; I will not kill my sisters like she wants." Zanderley pulled her knees up to her chest making the chain rattle as it slid across the wood. Placing her cheek on her knees she looked out the window. Then remembering the spell, she quietly moved and took the spell out to read it. Zanderley made a mental note on the ingredients for the spell. Then on the very bottom of the page she noticed there was writing she did not notice before. To make this a sleeping spell, substitute chamomile in place of deadly nightshade. A slow grin spread across her face, folding the spell she put it back where it was hiding. Wanting to see what her sisters were doing she took the tiny vile that Apollo gave her. Checking on Morgana one last time to make sure it was safe she picked up her cup of water and sprinkled some in. Nothing happened, feeling defeated she hung her head and said, "I just wanted to see my sisters." The water started to ripple and then Temprance and Acelyn came into view. Taking one hand she covered her mouth to quiet the sobs while she watched her sister pack bags and talk about her.

"Come on guys, grab what you need we are wasting daylight. She needs us and we need her. Who knows if Morgana has hurt her?" said Acelyn. Temprance looked over at her sister and said, "Do not worry Ace, we will get Zanderley and then the three of us will give that bitch something to think about."

Hearing that Morgana was waking up, she stuck her finger in the water to make the vision disappear. Before Morgana could look, she dumped the water out of the window and sat the cup down. Morgana walked over to Zanderley and with an oily smile she said, "Good morning my pet, I will go out and get us some food before we work on your spell." Morgana turned on her heel and left the hut. While Morgana was out Zanderley moved quickly to put her plan in motion.

With Zanderley doing what she could on her end, Acelyn and Temprance rushed out of the castle with the others. Standing in the courtyard Acelyn asked, "Which way do we go?"

Jewel spoke up and said, "We were told that Morgana's hut was in the Desiccated Woods. So, we need to head South East, past the Dead Lands and through the Hallowed Woods."

Looking at the guys Jaz asked, "What do you think will be our best way of travel?" A voice came from behind them causing them all to jump. "I do not suggest flying, you do not want Morgana to know you are coming." When they turned around, they all yelled, "Artemis." Jewel ran and hugged her dear friend. "Oh, I am so glad you are okay." Artemis chuckled, "Remember my friend, I am a God. I am glad you all called my father, by him taking me to Mount Olympus I healed much faster."

Acelyn walked over to the beautiful Goddess and asked, "Are you here to help us find our sister?"

"No, sweet princess, I am here to give you a blessing from the Gods and this," said Artemis holding out a staff. Walking up to Artemis, Coda reached out and took the staff from her. "I will make sure it is safe until it is handed to Princess Zanderley," said Coda confidently.

Temprance studied the staff and asked, "Why does it just look like a stick and nothing like ours?" Turning to face Temprance Coda spoke, "It is a protection enchantment. It will show what it truly looks like after Zanderley holds onto it." With a proud smile Artemis nodded in agreement. "Now, for your blessing," said Artemis while opening her arms wide:

> The Olympian Twelve hear my plea,
> Bestow a blessing on these heroes,
> Help them see through the dark magic,
> Make it so they can see Princess Zanderley.

Artemis's eyes went pure white with sparks of electricity popping and snaping. Tipping her head back she lifted off the ground about four feet. The sky turned a dark gray and eleven lightning bolts hit the ground circling the heroes. Then Artemis lowered back to the ground and took her place in the circle next to her brother Apollo. The heroes looked at the Gods that surrounded them and all at once they knelt to show respect. Then the Gods started their blessing. When they spoke, it was all at once then each God gave their own blessing.

> May our blessings help you in your quest to find Princess Zanderley,
> **Zeus:** "May you have the speed of the Gods."
> **Hara:** "May you have the wisdom of the Gods."
> **Poseidon:** "May you have the strength of the sea."
> **Demeter:** "May you have the stealth of the wind."
> **Athena:** "May you have the knowledge of battle."
> **Apollo:** "May you have the knowledge of your enemy."
> **Artemis:** "May you have skill of the hunt."
> **Ares:** "May you have the heart of a warrior."
> **Hades:** "May you have the knowledge to replenish."
> **Aphrodite:** "May you have the compassion of the Gods."
> **Hermes:** "May you be light on your feet."

Dionysus: "May you have the knowledge of what is poison."
All: "It shall be done."

When the Gods finished their blessing, they felt a glow start in their hearts and spread until their whole body was warm. Just as quickly as they appeared, they were gone except for Apollo and Artemis. The Gods walked over to the heroes then Apollo spoke, "I have told the Princess that you are coming." Apollo nodded and he was gone, Artemis placed a hand on Acelyn's and Temprance's shoulders and spoke, "Be careful and move quickly," and with a wink and a smirk she was gone.

Acelyn turned and shouldered her pack and said, "Let's go get Zanderley." Picking up and shouldering his pack Anton joined Acelyn and waited for the others to join them. With their newfound courage and hearts full of love they took to their first landmark, The Dead Lands.

Chapter Thirty

Nightwing flew as steady as he could so the little fire fairy could sleep. When he saw Kane and Catarina at the cave entrance he spoke softly, "Ember, we are here." Ember stretched and rolled over the wrong way and fell.

Letting out a scream she fluttered her wings and landed softly next to Catarina. Embarrassed all she could do was smile and wave at Kane and Catarina and say, "We are here to help you free The Sisters of Fate." Bending down so she could see Ember better she asked, "And what is your name, little one?" asked Catarina.

Ember fluttered her wings, so her feet barely brushed the dirt on the ground, she held out her hand and said, "My name is Ember; it is nice to meet you, Miss Catarina. Oh, and this is Nightwing."

"How do you know my name, Ember?" asked Catarina. "It is nice to meet you and thank you for coming to help us."

Kane and the woodland gnome came over to great the newcomers. The woodland gnome spoke up, "She knows your name because of me, Miss Catarina, we are friends." When Ember saw the woodland gnome she squeaked and yelled, "Norman, you are safe." Unable to control herself she flew into him knocking him to the ground. "Ember, get up please I cannot breathe," Norman squeaked out. Moving quickly, she stood and offered Norman a hand up. "I am just so glad you are okay. How did you escape the curse?" asked Ember.

"Well, when Mya asked me to go and help Mr. Kane and Miss Catarina, I said yes. So, they keep me safe," explained Norman.

Kane looked up and noticed the sun was high in the sky, "We are running out of time, come on we need to hurry." Looking back at the boulder Kane asked, "Nightwing do you think you can push it out of the way?" Nodding Nightwing walked over to the boulder and placed his head in the middle of the boulder and pushed. The mountain started to shake, and a deep rumbling sound came from the bolder that was being slid. Looking up Ember noticed what was causing the mountain to shake. She yelled, "Nightwing, look up we have a problem."

Nightwing looked up and what he saw caused terror to flow down his spine. He had caused an avalanche of boulders and rocks. Knowing that his friends could not move fast enough to get away, he took his tail and neck and pulled everyone under him. Tucking his head underneath he used his wings to shield them from the falling boulders and rocks.

The sound of the falling rocks sounded like it was raining dirt. Just when it was almost over Nightwing let out a blood curdling cry that scared Ember and the others. Closing his eyes Nightwing sent a message to Ember telepathically, "Ember, get everyone out. I cannot hold the boulder for much longer." Looking around for an opening Ember noticed that Nightwing's legs were shaking from the weight of the boulder and rocks.

Seeing there was sliver of sunlight by his back right leg she said, "Come on everyone, help me push; we need to get out of here. Nightwing's strength will not hold out much longer." With them all working together and with a little bit of magic they were able to move Nightwing's wing just enough so they could escape. Letting out a soft whimper Nightwing's legs gave out and he collapsed. Quickly assessing to see how they could help the poor dragon, there was a boulder almost the size of Nightwing on his back. Catarina noticed that his right wing was broken, and the webbing of his wings were torn to shreds. Letting out a cry Ember flew over to her friend and with her tiny hand she gripped the tip of his horn and tried to pull his head out from under his leg. Kane joined Ember and tried to help; Catarina wrapped her arms around her middle and wept. Norman started moving the rock from around Nightwing's battered wings.

The more Ember pulled the more frustrated she got. Ember let out a scream and her wings transformed in to dark red and black flames. With one last tug Ember and Kane pulled the unconscious dragon's head out from under his leg. Spreading her arms Ember hugged Nightwing's snout and with tears falling she flew above the boulder that was pinning him down. With all the sorrow and anger she held inside she cupped her hands and conjured a glowing red orb. Slowly Kane backed up to stand with the others and watched the angry fire fairy. They watched as Ember slowly spread her hands apart to where the orb was hovering. When Ember's eyes turned crimson he said, "Come on guys we need to back up, there is no telling how powerful she is going to make that orb."

As they backed up Ember spread her arms increasing the gap, the bigger the gap got the bigger the orb grew. She put her arms down to her sides and the orb slowly spun. With a quick movement of her hand, it was like she cut the strings of a marionette. The orb fell onto the boulder causing it to explode and rain rock pieces on her friends.

When it was safe, Catarina ran to Nightwing to see what she could do in help in healing him. She ran her hands over his battered and tattered wings, she took a deep breath and as loud as she could she summoned Dionysus for help.

Hail Dionysus hear my plea,
Help us heal this dragon,
So that we my free The Sisters of Fate.
And help the sisters three complete their destiny
So, mote it be.

The clouds grew dark and the wind stirred the loose dirt creating dust devils. The ground shook making the rocks tremble. With a bright flash of light, the air crackled with electricity and when the dust settled there stood Dionysus.

Dionysus looked at the group that was huddled around the broken dragon. With a booming voice he asked, "What could be so important to put you in the debt with the Gods?"

Still filled with her anger Ember flew up to eye level, putting her hands on her hips and bending at the waist she spoke. "How dare you come down here and have that kind of attitude when we are trying to save your world? You need to learn how to show us just a little bit of respect."

"Listen little one you need to watch your tone when speaking to a God."

"No, you need to learn that we have feelings, and your world does revolve around us. Plus, if we choose, we could let this world die and if it dies so do you."

The God crossed his arms and studied the tiny fire fairy. "You have fire in your soul, little one. You seem so fierce and strong for a tiny thing. What can I do to help you little warrior?" asked Dionysus.

"You can heal our friend," said Ember pointing behind her to Nightwing.

Dionysus unfolded his arms and walked over to Nightwing and laid his hand on his neck. Looking back at the others he said, "Your friend has been gravely injured, not only has his wings been destroyed his back is broken. I will need your help, little warrior, to heal him."

"What can we do to help?" asked Catarina.

Looking at Kane, Catarina, Norman, and Ember he said, "You can all help by placing your hands on Nightwing and picture in your mind healing his injuries," said Dionysus.

Dionysus waited until everyone was touching Nightwing. Then he blinked his eyes and lifted off the ground, his eyes turned to static and the wind picked up. Reaching to the sky he turned it into night and called down a star. When Dionysus held the star in his hand he floated back to the ground. Walking over to Nightwing he pressed the star into Nightwing's chest. The others watched as the light from the star moved throughout his body to his injuries. When the light made it to the webbing of the wings, they all watched with amazement when the rips in his wings started to mend. When the healing was done Ember gasped. It looked like he never took a hit with boulders or rocks. Going with the feeling in her heart, Ember flew into Dionysus once again but this time she bent at the waist and kissed the tip of his nose. With the sweetest smile she said, "Thank you, he got hurt saving our lives."

Looking at the mountain Dionysus asked, "What were you doing?"

Kane spoke up, "Nightwing was trying to move the boulder that is blocking the entrance to the cave that holds The Sisters of Fate. We are here to free them from stone. Luna, Star, and Night sent us because Morgana has kidnaped one of the princesses."

"Yes, I just left the young queens; they are headed to find their sister. Let us wake up Nightwing and get him out of the way of the door and I will see what I can do to help," said Dionysus. Walking over and placing his hand on Nightwing's snout in a soft voice he spoke, "Mighty Fire dragon, it is time to wake there is work to be done." A puff of red smoke came from Nightwing's snout and his eyes fluttered open. With a squeal of delight Ember flew in a circle and then landed on Nightwing's snout.

Finding his strength Nightwing stood, he extended his wings, and shook all the debris off him and looked at everyone. "How is this possible, I thought I was going to die?"

"Because brave dragon, your quest does not end here. You are destined to do great things," said Dionysus. Nightwing lowered his head so he could look Dionysus in the eyes. Tipping his head from side to side he studied the God. He noticed Dionysus is over seven-feet tall with dark chestnut brown wavy hair that is past his shoulders and he wore a crown made from grape vines. The crown is embellished with tri-colored grape leaves and the most delicious red, green, and purple grapes. His skin is a golden tan, and every muscle is defined. He wore a purple tunic that clasped over his right shoulder with a gold grape leaf securing the knot. The tunic came to just above his knees and his boots were made from leather with grape vines burned into them. Around his waist was a leather strap that held a clay jug full of wine. The most captive thing about the God of Wine is his eyes. Instead of his being white like the other Gods, Dionysus's eyes were the color of a good Merlot.

"What are you thinking about, brave dragon?" asked Dionysus.

"Not to be rude or any disrespect but I was wondering why they called you to heal me and not Apollo?" asked Nightwing.

"Because all of us can heal and Apollo has helped way too much already. Every time a god comes down here, Morgana can tell it. The last time Apollo was here he was almost detected. We need to hurry so I can get back. Brave dragon, if you would move, I will see what I can do to open the cave entrance."

When everyone was safely out of the way, Dionysus stretched out his arms and rose off the ground. He spun in a circle picking up speed until the clouds turned dark and gray. After Dionysus was back on the ground the air seemed to pulse around him. Then he reached to the sky and caught a lightning bolt in his hand. He spun in a circle and threw the lightning bolt like a javelin and hit the boulder in the center, causing it to explode into dust. When the dust settled Dionysus looked back at the group nodded his head then disappeared.

Chapter Thirty-One

The group studied the cave opening, there was a strange blue glow coming from inside. Catarina clung to Kane and asked, "I wonder where that is coming from?"

"I do not know, my love."

Ember was the first to enter the cave with the others following close behind her. The deeper in the cave they went the glow seemed to pulse. Catarina noticed that the cave looked different than the rest of Aadya. Confused she walked up to the wall and when she touched it, she discovered that the walls were seeping water. "Kane, come check this out," said Catarina without looking back. When she felt Kane standing next to her, she asked, "Do you think the reason the cave is different than all of Aadya is because the curse is weakening?"

"We have no way to tell if it is the curse weakening or if this place was only partially affected because of the amount of magic here," said Kane.

"We need to hurry because if the curse has weakened, we do not know what lurks in the dark," commented Ember causing everyone to turn and look at her.

The cave looked like it was a gateway to the Underworld only instead of it being warm and smelling like brimstone, it was cold, damp, and smelled musty. As they moved forward, they noticed the cracks in the walls from the avalanche earlier. Just as Ember was about to cross over the threshold into a large room a human size stalactite fell almost impaling Ember and blocking the entrance to the room. Letting out a squeak she flew and hid on Nightwing's back. So Nightwing went over to the stalactite and opening his massive jaws he picked it up and moved off to the side. Using his tail so no one could pass he looked up to make sure no more were going to fall. When he was sure it was safe, he stretched his neck to investigate the next room. Then he backed out and looked down at Kane, Catarina, and Norman and nodded his head letting them know it was safe for them to enter. Catarina was the first to notice that the glow was coming from the Sisters of Fate. They gathered around the Sisters of Fate and watched as the glow would go from a light glow to a glow so bright it looked like it was coming from a star.

Catarina walked up to the first sister and spoke. "I know you all know them as the Sisters of Fate, but do you know what their names are and what they do?" When she looked back everyone was shaking their head no. She turned her head back to look at the first sister and spoke. "This is the oldest and her name is Atropos also known as the inflexible one. She is the sister that finalizes your fate even sometimes causing death by cutting the thread that represents a human's fate and life. She is exceptionally beautiful in her own way. Atropos has long raven black hair that touches her feet. She wears a gold head piece that has mother of pearl in the shape of an eye that rests on her forehead. Her eyes are black and there is no white visible. Her skin is the color of alabaster with zero flaws. The gown she is wearing is long and drags on the ground as she walks. The corset of the gown is made of gold, from the corset to the bottom of the gown is colored from deep purple to black."

Walking over to the middle sister she continued. "This is Lachesis also known as the measurer. She is the one that determines your destiny (the thread that is spun for your life.) She has been known to show up within three days of a child being born to decide that child's fate. Lachesis is also unbelievably beautiful. She has long golden hair that touches her feet and her eyes are red like a ruby. Lachesis's gown is black with a crimson and gold corset. All the sisters wear a black cloak, but Lachesis never takes hers off because it hides her identity. Everyone meets Lachesis once in their life but because they are so young, they never remember.

"Now finally this is the youngest sister, and her name is Clotho. She is also known as the spinner. Clotho has the power to bring someone back to the land of the living if they have been wrongly accused. She is also the one that spins the thread of life. She is devastatingly beautiful. She has walnut brown hair that tumbles past her waist. Her eyes are orange with a red spiral pattern in them. She wears a cloth top made into two triangles that covers her breasts which is secured by leather straps. The belt that holds up her floor length covering is leather and gold. The covering is in two panels and the outside of her legs and hips are bare, the colors of the cloth is maroon and teal. Her boots are made from leather and they go up to her knees. She also carries the Spear of Destiny."

Catarina turned and looked at the group, "The reason I am telling you all of this is when we free them you must show them the utmost respect. That means you Ember, no back talking them, they hold your future in their hands. So please show them the respect they deserve." Now looking very tired Catarina walked over to Kane and laid her head on his shoulder when he wrapped his arm around her. Flying in front of Nightwing's face Ember said, "Okay, I guess we are up. Now remember you can do this just have a little faith." Nodding Nightwing took in a deep breath and sent out a jet of white and crimson flames.

When Nightwing was done the only sound, you could hear was the sound of cracking stone. The group watched in amazement as the life slowly came back into the Sisters of Fate. Cracks started at their feet and ran up their bodies making it look like veins. The bigger the cracks go the brighter the blue glow shined. Then slowly the stone started to fall away revealing what was underneath.

The Sisters of Fate took their first breath in centuries and opened their eyes to see who freed them. Stepping free of the debris at their feet the Sisters of Fate walked circles around the group. Nightwing remembering at the last minute bowed his head in respect. The others noticed and dropped to one knee and bowed their heads not saying a word. Clotho stopped in front of Catarina and took the Spear of Destiny and placed it under her chin and slowly lifted Catarina's face to meet hers. When one of the sisters spoke, it sounded like all three were speaking at once, their voices had a mystical sound that echoed around them.

"Where are the young Queens? Why are they not here? Why was it you that freed us?"

Catarina looked into her mystic swirling eyes and spoke the truth, "Luna, Star, and Night sent us to free you from the curse because things have changed. Morgana has kidnaped Princess Zanderley. Princess Acelyn and Princess Temprance with the dragon guardians are on their way to go and rescue her." The

Sisters of Fates' eyes went wide, and they went to a clear spot in the room and made a circle by holding hands and called for their Calling Waters.

Calling Waters come to thee
Because we need to see
Someone had tried to change their destiny
Come to us and
Let us see
Let us see
So that the three
Queens can fulfill
Their destiny
So, mote it be.

The blue light that was just a dim glow grew so bright it caused the group to close and shield their eyes. When Kane opened his eyes the sight before him caused him to take a step back. The room had completely changed. It was just an empty room in a cave where the Sisters of Fate rested in stone. Now it is their workshop, where there is a black cauldron with a crackling fire under it. Cabinets and shelves filled the once empty walls. They held jars that were full to the top and some were empty. In the center of the chamber sat three thrones that were covered in animal fur. A shallow stone well with water that seemed to have a life of its own sat in front of the thrones. Ember flew higher so she could turn and see the whole room. She let out a "wow" under her breath when she saw that the floors were made from a mirror like material. Looking up at Ember, Atropos gave her a knowing smirk then looked back at the moving water.

Without looking up the Sisters spoke, "Come and have a look in our Calling Waters." As the others approached the shallow well, they watched as past events played. When they watched the battle outside the castle the first night the Princesses were in Aadya. The Sisters of Fate nodded their heads and looked at each other. When the waters went black, they looked up at the group and spoke.

"The young Queens are showing much courage and if they stay on the path that they are on, they will make wonderful Queens. The path may have shifted a little, but they are right where they need to be. Now we have questions for you. Who found Queen Bella? Where is she now?"

Stepping forward Ember answered, "Princess Temprance is the one who found Queen Bella. Queen Bella decided to help on her own, and she is with Kahn." Holding up a hand to stop Ember from saying more they waved their hand over the water and once again watched the past. When the water turned black, they looked up at Ember. "Explain little one, do you believe that this will work? Do you honestly believe that the darkness can be extracted out of Kahn's heart?"

Folding her hands in front of her she fluttered her wings and flew just a little closer. "Yes, I do, because of the love that they share I believe love will win. Kahn may like the power he wields; but he loves Bella more."

The Sisters of Fate looked at each other and seemed to be having a conversation without talking. This went on for several minutes then they looked at the group and nodded. Clotho stood and walked closer to Catarina, Kane, Ember, Norman, and Nightwing. Then they spoke, "If you want Bella and the young Queens to win this war your next step is to find our sisters. Luna, Star, and Night will be expecting you. We have given you a blessing of invisibility. Now you may travel and make camp without being seen by what hunts you. Now go!!"

As soon as they finished speaking the room in the cave was empty once again except for the lingering blue glow to give a little light. Not knowing how fast the glow would die Norman said, "Come on guys let us get out of here while we can still see. Or before they change their mind and come back and cut all of our threads." Then he took off at a brisk pace for the cave entrance.

When everyone was outside Kane looked to the sky and noticed that it was almost dusk. Looking at the others he spoke, "Hey it is going to be dark soon and I do not think it is safe to camp here. The Sisters of Fate said the blessing would hide us. I do not want to take the chance that the smell of a campfire would go unnoticed my one of Morgana's minions. Just in case she sends one by to check that the cave has been untouched and still sealed."

"Ember, where do we need to go?" asked Catarina.

"We need to head to the Emerald Sea, that is where the ritual will take place to free Kahn."

"Miss Catarina and Mr. Kane, you may ride on my back, she does not need to be walking," said Nightwing.

Everyone watched as Nightwing laid down and extended his wing so Catarina and Kane could climb on his back. Once she was settled, she looked down at Norman and held her arms open welcoming him into them. Norman climbed up and sat down in front of Catarina looking back he said, "Thank you, Miss Cat."

Nightwing took off and flew south to meet up with the others. When they were almost out of sight Catarina looked back at the cave and watched as Clotho waved her hand at the mountain closing off the entrance once again.

Chapter Thirty-Two

In the run-down hut in the Desiccated Woods, Zanderley was doing everything she could to stall Morgana's plans. Zanderley was reading through the pile of dusty and stained spell books that Morgana had placed on the table when Morgana spoke, "Stay here pretty princess, while I go and get us supplies."

Worried, all Zanderley could do is look at her and nod knowing she was going to get terribly upset when she noticed that Death was gone. Zanderley kept her nose in the book with her thoughts, hoping that they were hers and Morgana could not know what she was thinking. "I want to run but Apollo and Hades both said for me to wait for my sisters. But I know if I wait for them Morgana is going to make me do something horrible to them or worse...."

Zanderley heard Morgana mumble to herself while gathering her dingy burlap satchel. When she left, she slammed the door and called for her pet. "Spike, watch over our princess do not let her escape or let anyone in," said Morgana with a snarling voice while turning to look where the pup had been laying. Morgana let out a growl that confirmed Zanderley's suspicions that Morgana was part demon. "Where did that worthless thing go? How did he get free?" Then Zanderley heard her speak in a different language and saw a shimmering circle surround the hut. She watched Morgana disappear into the woods.

Zanderley watched out the window to make sure Morgana was truly gone and just not hiding to see if she would try and escape. When Zanderley felt like the coast was clear she quickly moved over to the door and pulled it open.

Her heart felt like it was beating out of her chest. "Maybe if I can get away, I can meet up with my sisters." Checking her surroundings one more time she took off. Zanderley was knocked on her ass from the electrical charge from the barrier that was keeping her in the hut. Zanderley had tears in her eyes as she picked herself up off the ground. She slammed the door shut then stomping back to the table she plopped herself down in front of the stack of books. "I hope my sisters get here soon. I really do not want to hurt them. But if she makes me do a spell, I know one that will work."

Acelyn watched the shadows as the heroes made their way across Aadya to the Desiccated Woods. She had the feeling that they were being watched from what lurked in the shadows, so she leaned in and spoke softly to Anton, "Keep point I am going fall back and talk to Tempie." With a nod Anton kept watch as Acelyn stopped and waited for her sister and Jewel to catch up. Placing herself between the two she asked so only they could hear, "Do you guys feel like we are being watched?"

Grabbing her sister's arm Temprance spoke, "Yes, we were just talking about that. Jaz, Zeke, and Coda told us to move into the center of the group just in case what is watching us is out to harm us."

Before Acelyn or Jewel could comment on what Temprance said they noticed the guys had closed in the ranks making Acelyn, Temprance, and Jewel safe in the center. Acelyn caught movement out of the corner of her eye so she placed her hand on the hilt of her sword. Still speaking just above a whisper, "Did you two see that?" tipping her head in the direction she saw the movement. Just as Temprance was about to answer she saw the movement, she put her finger up to her lips making sure everyone stayed quiet. Temprance kept her eyes on where the movement was coming from as she pulled her bow from around her shoulders. Reaching behind her, she grabbed one of the arrows from the quiver and notched it in the bow. Pulling the bow string tight she lifted the bow and waited for movement.

As soon as Temprance saw movement she let her arrow fly. From the shadows they all heard a yowl that caused everyone to cover their ears. Knowing that they would never outrun whatever was hunting them, they stood their ground hoping that they could handle whatever came for them. Out of the shadows came a creature that made her bones want to shake with fear.

The creature had a human head with glowing blue and red eyes and very sharp pointy teeth. It had the body of a lion and fur that was auburn and black, and its tail reminded Acelyn of a scorpion's tail. Pulling her sword out of its sheath she asked, "What the hell is that?" Before anyone could answer the creature lunged and swiped his claws across Zeke's chest knocking Zeke to the ground. Before anyone could react a beautiful black bird with long flowing feathers came in and landed on the creature's back digging his talons in. Turning his head, he looked at the group, "Hurry run! You all will be safe when you are in the boundaries of the Dead Lands."

Acelyn stood guard with her sword at the ready while Temprance shifted and the others lifted a bleeding and unconscious Zeke on her back. Acelyn's heart clutched and felt like it was in her chest when she saw the tail of the creature heading for the bird that came to their aid. Acting on instinct Acelyn swung her sword and sliced the creature's tail off. The bird turned its head and said, "GO. NOW!" Seeing that the bird was on even ground she nodded at him and took off with the others.

Once in the Dead Lands Acelyn helped lift Zeke and lay him on the ground. Her heart bled for seeing her sister in pain. Tears silently fell down her cheeks as she watched Jaz work on Zeke. It seemed to be taking an extremely long time to heal his wounds, just as Acelyn thought it was helpless, the bird showed up. Acelyn studied this bird and prayed it was on their side.

This beautiful, majestic bird is the same height as Acelyn. His eyes are the same color violet as Temprance. Mesmerized by the color of his feathers she lifted her hand and stroked the black/purple feathers. After feeling how soft and silky they were she ran her hand from the nape of his neck to about the middle of his back. That is when the vision of the past took hold....

It was a warm fall afternoon when Natalia took Malic out to the courtyard to pay. There was a slight breeze with the scent of Autumn. Natalia sat on one of the stone benches and watched three-year-old Malic play. Malic climbed on the bench across from Natalia and stood taking his wooden sword and said excitedly, "Natalia, I am going be king one day like Father."

"Yes, young Prince you will be a great King one day. But you must make sure you can best someone in a duel. So young Prince may I suggest that you practice on your sword combat," said Natalia with a wide smile.

Nodding excitedly Malic jumped off the bench and ran into the courtyard and challenged every bush that he came by with a duel. While Natalia watched the young prince, she also noticed the leaves changing colors, and how the castle was busy with servants some decorating inside the castle and the rest decorating outside. Neither the young Prince nor Natalia knew the danger that just lurked just on the outskirts of the castle grounds.

A massive black panther with a cloaked rider crept closer to the grounds. Just on the edge in the shadows the cloaked rider sang a siren's song luring the young Prince to the shadows. Natalia was daydreaming and never noticed when the young Prince wandered off into the woods. When Malic reached the panther and rider he was fully enthralled and made no noise when the rider reached down and picked him up. When the rider had him seated on the panther, they took off far away from the castle.

When Queen Anastasia came out to play with her little boy, she saw no sight of him anywhere. "Natalia, where is my son?" Noticing that Natalia was not moving, and her eyes were clouded over she placed a hand on her shoulder. When there was still no response, the Queen placed the palm of her hand on Natalia's head and said, "Clear." Natalia's vision cleared and she shook her head then looked up to the Queen. With her eyes going wide she dropped to her knees and said, "Oh, my Queen, what may I do for you?"

Anastasia clasped her hands in front of her and asked once again but this time sounded a little panicked, "Where is my son?"

Standing up quickly she pointed in the direction she had last seen Malic, "Over there......" her voice trailed off not seeing the young Prince.

Not knowing what happen to her son and with the war between the dragons and with Kahn, Queen Anastasia took no chances. Looking at Natalia she said, "Go and ring the alarm bell I will go and tell Alexzander what has happened. Falling to her knees and bowing Natalia started weeping and said, "I am sorry I have failed you. I do not know what happened he was playing, and I do not remember anything else until you talked to me."

Crouching down Anastasia pulled the weeping woman up from the ground then she lifted her head so she could look at her in the eyes. "You were under a spell, there was nothing that you could have done to prevent this. But you can help now, go and do what I said. There is still time to find the Prince. NOW GO!"

Holding her dress so that she would not trip on it she ran to the castle. When entering the castle, she never slowed, her footsteps echoed throughout the castle. When she made it to the King's writing room, she forcefully pushed open the doors causing the room to echo and shake.

King Alexzander looked up from his work and looked into the frightened eyes of his wife. Standing he met her halfway, enveloping her in his arms he

Return to Aadya

tried to sooth her. All she could say before the alarm bell rang was, "Malic is gone." Looking up the King looked at his guards and said, "One of you fetch Natalia the other ready mine and the queen's horses."

Shaking her head, she pulled away from Alexzander and said, "It will be faster if I shift and you ride. In my liger form I am faster and stronger than any horse."

"Very well Anna, let us go we need to hurry."

Outside the castle King Alexzander readied his army. "The prince is missing. At this point we believe he was taken because his nurse maid was placed under a spell. Now go and find the Prince."

Just as they were about to leave a guard yelled that there was someone coming, and they are carrying a sack. Sniffing Anastasia scented blood and took off. At the edge of the drawbridge Anastasia stopped and Alexzander climbed down, and she shifted. They waited for the cloaked person to get close enough. Anastasia's heart was pounding then she noticed the tiny bloody arm that bounced with every step. If it were not for the guards Anastasia would have ran right into Morgana's plans. The sack was dropped, and the cloaked figure disappeared in smoke.

One of the guards bent down and cut the sack open revealing the bloody lifeless body of Prince Malic. King Alexzander turned Anastasia away from the body of their son. Holding her tight she wept on his shoulder while he tried to contain his rage. He whispered softly to her while he watched the guards search the body. His whole body vibrated with anger when he took the note found on Malic's body, opening the note he read....

If you have more children, this will be their fate. If you step down and give me the throne, I might let you live in a cell for the rest of your life. And I will take your queen as my own. If not, you shall die.

King Alexzander never questioned who killed Prince Malic; he always knew it was his brother. But what the King did not know is that Morgana was the one behind the killing of his son and not his brother. Shortly after Malic died, Apollo went to see his spirit in Elysian Fields and offered him another chance at life so that he may help his sisters when the time came. When Malic accepted Apollo made him the Dark Phoenix.

151

Chapter Thirty-Three

When the vision cleared Acelyn slid boneless to the ground and passed out. Temprance felt like she was being torn in two because she did not want to leave Zeke's side, but she knew her sister needed her. Malic looked at Temprance and said, "Help her, I will make sure your mate will be okay." Looking into Malic's eyes she felt she could trust this bird but had no idea why. Slowly she let go of Zeke's hand and joined the others around Acelyn.

Malic knew as soon as the vision took over Acelyn, he did not know what to do about it or what he was going to say to his sisters. He knew as soon as Acelyn woke up she would tell the others. Malic looked down on his sister's mate and knew he needed to save his life. Because if he died, so would Temprance. Malic leaned his head over the gashes in Zeke's chest and tipped his head sideways and blinking a couple of times he dropped tears in the gashes. Malic watched as the gashes slowly closed, and he would drop another tear on them when needed. When Zeke was fully healed, he turned so he could see his sisters. Temprance was sitting with Acelyn's head in her lap and was stroking her hair away from her face. Malic lowered his head and whispered into her ear, "Time to wake up, little sister."

Acelyn's eyes fluttered then opened and her eyes locked onto Malic. Slowly she got to her feet. Without any word she flung her arms around Malic's neck. He lowered and rested his head on top of Acelyn's head. Wondering what was going on, Temprance looked at the others and shock was on everyone's face except for Jewel's.

"Jewel, why is Acelyn acting like that?" asked Temprance

"It is not for me to say. Just put it this way if you knew what Acelyn did, you would be the same way."

That got everyone's attention and looked at Jewel.

"What is going on, Jewel?" asked a very frustrated Anton.

Jewel looked at Malic and saw his nod, so she turned to Temprance placing a hand on her arm. With a smile and tears in her eyes she said, "Temprance, this is Malic."

Before Jewel cold finish the sentence Malic said, "I am your brother."

While Temprance and Acelyn were in the Dead Lands, Zanderley was casting a spell hoping that it would just put her sisters to sleep and not kill them. Malic felt Acelyn go limp and fall to the ground once again. The others watched in horror as Anton shortly followed. Jewel tried to catch Temprance as she fell next to Acelyn. Jewel dropped to her knees and placed her hands on their foreheads and looked up at everyone and said, "They're under a sleeping spell. That means Anton and Zeke have been affected as well. What do we do now? We cannot wake them without their Princess Zanderley."

Coda looked at his fallen brothers and their mates, "This must be the work of Morgana."

"I do not think it was Morgana. I think this was something else," explained Jaz.

Malic puffed up his chest, "All of you are needed to rescue my sister, I will watch over them. I promise no harm will come to them here."

"No, Jewel and Jaz need to stay here with them. I will go and rescue the princess. Please I need to do this so that I may redeem myself," said Coda shouldering his pack. Looking at the sleeping princesses one more time he spoke, "Just keep them safe, I will be back with Princess Zanderley soon." Then Coda took off at a jog in the direction of the Desiccated Woods. Moving as quickly as he could Coda made sure he always kept an eye on his surroundings.

Zanderley sat at the table silently weeping and praying to the Gods that she did not just kill her sisters. Morgana sat a bowl of water in front of Zanderley. She watched as Morgana called to see the princesses. She let the tears slid down her cheeks as he looked upon her sisters laying on the ground still as death.

Morgana looked at Zanderley with glee in her eyes knowing she has almost achieved her revenge on the royal line. Lifting Zanderley's face so she could look into her eyes she smiled and said, "Well pretty Princess I only have you, Kahn, and Bella left to deal with. Then my revenge on your royal family blood will be complete."

"What do you mean?" asked a weepy Zanderley.

"Well my dear, this all started thousands of years ago when King Alexzander the first hung my mother for the use of black magic. I was only fifteen years old when the king made me an orphan. That is when I made a vow that I would search and find the power I needed to achieve my revenge and end your royal blood line. Then I would take over the castle and rule all of Aadya."

"So, you had me kill my sisters to take over Aadya?"

"No princess it started long before. Would you like to hear your family history?" asked Morgana.

Figuring that if she were going to destroy Morgana, she needed all the information she could get. Slowly she nodded and kept a close eye on Morgana as she moved around the hut.

"It all started when King Nickoli and his wife Queen Tatianna had trouble conceiving a child. So, they searched all Aadya for a sorceress to help the queen conceive a child. Because of what the king's father did to my mother no one would help. So I waited months until I sent a message to the king saying I would help. When they came to see me, I did what I said I would help with, I just made sure it would help me along the way. I made sure that the child she carried had a dark seed of evil in his heart.

"In the Autumn, the queen gave birth to twin boys. I never expected for her to have twins. Thus, she did, and their names are Alexzander and Kahn. It took a lot longer than expected but finally I had gained control of one of the twins. Just after Alexzander and Kahn married their queens, I was able to have Kahn defy the Gods by drinking the blood of dragons and sealing his fate. When I was making Kahn power hungry his beloved Bella escaped Aadya and hid in Edan out of my sight. Then King Alexzander and Queen Anastasia had a child. His name was Malic. I waited until the young prince turned three before I lured him into the woods with a siren's song. I let my hell hound play with him like a chew toy, then I poisoned the young prince. After the prince was dead, I put on a hooded cloak and carried him back to the castle myself. I reveled in the look on the King and Queen's faces when they realized that it was their precious young prince. I left a note with the body of the young prince blaming everything on the King's brother.

"When Kahn started wondering where his beloved Bella was, I told him that his brother, King Alexzander, had her killed because of what happed to the young prince. This enraged Khan so much all he needed was just little suggestions. When he found out that the queen was with child once again, he started making plans for the curse that was Aadya's demise. The queen gave birth to three girls, and their names are Temprance Jade (first born), Acelyn (second born), and Zanderley (third born). When the princesses were three days old, Kahn went to the castle to kill you and your sisters. Instead he found Luna, Star, and Night sending you and your sisters somewhere Kahn would never be able to find you. Kahn was in such a rage because his brother bested him once again, he turned on his own blood and killed the king and queen. We found out much later that the three princesses could break the curse and save Aadya.

"So, we waited and helped Kahn gain more and more power, we also searched out answers on when you three would be back. The prophecy said that the three princesses needed to start their journey to find each other one month before their twenty-third birthday. Then they would make their way back home to Aadya with the help of three dragon guardians. With forming bonds that are stronger than family they would fight the war against the great evil that was destroying Aadya.

"There you have it my dear princess, I have stopped the prophecy with you helping me. You see I was not strong enough to destroy your sisters on my own since Bella had come back and weakened my hold on Khan. So, you will help me destroy Kahn and Bella then you will take your place as Queen and after your coronation you will announce me as your royal advisor. Then I will finally have all Aadya bowing at my feet." Morgana watched as the hope died in Zanderley's eyes and she smiled showing all her sharp teeth. "So does your smart mouth have anything to say?"

"I only have one. What are you going to do when you get old? There will be someone that can destroy you."

Tipping her head back she laughed, "Silly little princess, I will not grow old I am immortal. I am already thousands of years old. So, to answer your question I will never grow old."

"How are you immortal? You had a mother so that means you were born and not created."

"When my mother was killed, I told you I searched for power. When I was about to give up this creature came to me and offed its help. He said he

156

came from another realm and where he was from, he could offer me more power than was offered here. The creature was about eight-foot-tall, black leather skin with the biggest set of bat wings I had ever seen. His eyes were blood red and horns came from his head. His mouth was full of razor-sharp teeth and his tongue reminded me of a snake. His nails on his feet made sparks on the rocks when he walked, and the claws on his hand I swear were almost three inches long.

"I remember being terrified when I saw him, but I wanted the power more. He told me that I would have the power I wanted and would have immortality. The funny thing was he only wanted one thing from me, my soul, knowing if I gave him my soul, I would never end up in Tartarus, so it was a win, win for me."

Zanderley smirked and said, "You are truly a blooming idiot. You sold your soul to a demon. Which means you are truly damned. You may think you have escaped Hell or this realms version of it. All you did was get a demon's bastardized version of powers to make you feel like a God. Also, when that demon is tired of playing with you or no longer needed, he will pull his contract and you will die and go straight to hell. Do you want to know what happens to damned souls in Hell? Let me enlighten you. You will be put on what we call the rack and endure endless torture. That means demons can peel the skin off bones and when you think it will never end you will heal, and they will start all over again. So not even knowing it, you condemned yourself. Demons have the worst sense of humor, they will wait until you think you have everything you ever wanted and then pull the rug out from underneath you." Zanderley smiled and started clapping her hands, "Oh, I almost forgot; congratulations, Dumb Ass!"

Morgana was so mad she back handed Zanderley so hard it sent her flying backwards. When Zanderley opened her eyes and looked at Morgana she truly saw the demon inside. Just as Morgana reached down to pick up Zanderley she smelled smoke. Looking out the window she watched as her beloved Desecrated Woods go up in a blaze of flames. Running outside to try and stop the blaze, she forgot all about Zanderley and making sure she stayed in the hut.

Zanderley wiped the blood from her lip with the back of her hand and walked to the door. Putting a hand out in front of her she checked for the barrier but found none. She remembered her sisters and ran to the spell books quickly looking for the spell she needed. When Zanderley found it, she ripped it out of the book and shoved it in her pocket and took off. She headed to the black part of the burnout woods and saw a beautiful blue dragon. Hoping it was friendly she ran to it.

Coda watched Zanderley run with her sun kissed blonde hair flowing behind her. When she got close, he lowered his wing so she could climb on. When they were far enough away, he spoke. "Hello Princess, I am Coda. I am here to rescue you and take you to your sisters."

Chapter Thirty-Four

Coda was beyond happy that Zanderley was by his side that he was trembling. Coda could tell something was wrong when Zanderley went limp on his back. Not knowing what to do he flew as fast as he could to get her back to her sisters. As they flew Coda looked at his home, so much has changed already in the couple of days since the Princesses arrival. The Princesses are bringing Aadya back to life. Coda turned his head and looked at Zanderley and wondered if Anton and Zeke were right; was she his soulmate or would she choose someone else? He had only been with her a short time, but he could feel his soul starting to reach out to hers.

Seeing the others coming into sight Coda started his angling towards the ground making sure he did not let Zanderley fall. When he was close enough, he called for Jaz and Jewel, "Come and help me, halfway here she passed out."

"What happened to her?" asked Malic.

Jewel and Jaz lifted the princess off his back, and they laid her down next to her sisters. Malic looked at his sister and wept from sorrow, they did not look like they were sleeping. They looked like death, their skin was very pale, and their chests barely moved when they breathed. When a tear fell on Zanderley, Malic noticed that the ruby on her choker glowed.

"We need to get this chocker off her, it was put on by Morgana. I think this is why she is unconscious. Morgana makes these chokers so she can control anyone or thing," explained Malic.

"What do I need to do?" asked Coda.

"Here Coda, try some of this," said Jewel handing him a pouch.

Coda took the pouch from Jewel and opened it, inside he saw sand that shimmered and shined like tiny diamonds. Looking up at Jewel he asked, "What is this?"

"That is the pixie dust I used before my powers grew. All you need to do is take a pinch of it think about what you would like it to do then sprinkle it," she said with a smile.

Taking in a deep breath he sprinkled some in the palm of his hand and wished that the choker would come off. Putting his hands together he rubbed them, making the pixie dust sprinkle and land on the ruby. The ruby started to have a soft glow then it grew brighter and brighter until the ruby shattered. Morgana's magic started to fall away and what was left was the vine that she weaved her twisted magic around. Reaching down Coda grabbed the vine to pull it away from Zanderley's neck and it disintegrated into dust at his touch. The only evidence that was left behind was a faint red line from where the choker was too tight around her neck.

Everyone watched and waited for Zanderley to wake, it felt like an eternity. As soon as her eyes started to flutter everyone moved in closer just waiting for the pretty blue eyes to open. When her eyes finally opened, they locked onto Coda's and he felt his heart make a small roll in his chest feeling love for the first time.

Zanderley stared into his sea serpent green eyes trying to figure out why they seemed so familiar. She felt a strange pull in her belly. Feeling just a little bit uncomfortable she pushed herself to sit up. That is when she noticed the other two people and a huge black bird. Zanderley cleared her throat and let out a weak, "Hi, what happened to the dragon that saved me and who are you?"

Jaz was the first to speak, "Hello Princess my name is Jaz. This is Jewel, Coda, and the big bird is Malic. We watched over your sisters while Coda rescued you from Morgana."

Before anyone could utter another word, she turned her head franticly looking for her sisters. With her heart full of sorrow, she slowly moved to kneel between her sisters and placing a hand on each shoulder she hung her head in shame feeling like a failure and wept.

Feeling that he was already in sync with Zanderley he walked over to her and knelt behind her wrapping his arms safely around her trying to ease her pain. Speaking softly Coda talked to her, "Why all the tears, Princess?"

"Because I have failed them, I did the spell wrong. Instead of saving them I killed them," said Zanderley weeping even harder.

Malic moved over and stood in front of Zanderley and spoke, "Dear sweet Princess, you have not failed your sisters; they are only sleeping. You did the spell correctly, all they are waiting for is for you to wake them."

Zanderley knuckled away tears while trying to process what Malic was saying. Looking back down she watched Acelyn's chest slowly rise and fall, she did the same with Temprance. Zanderley reached in her pocket and pulled out the last spell she took from Morgana. Unfolding it she read:

To counter a sleeping curse

Ingredients:

Two drops of blood from the one under the curse
Two drops of blood from the caster
Pinch of pixie dust
A tear from a phoenix
Water from a spring

Incantation:

Hail to the Gods hear my plea,
Grant me the strength I need
So that I may wake my sisters from sleep
Remove this curse that I have placed on thee
So that we may fulfill our destiny
So, mote it be
Directions: Mix all Ingredients together until you get a paste
Mark an X on the forehead of the cursed with the paste

Say incantation then set leftover paste on fire

Looking up Zanderley asked, "Does anyone know where I can get these things?"

Taking the worn page from Zanderley Jewel read. Nodding she said, "Yes, I have the pixie dust, Malic is a phoenix, and there is a stream of spring water in Singing Fields and the rest comes from you and your sisters."

Letting out a sigh of relief she took the paper back and stood. Looking at the group of strangers she asked, "I know I do not know any of you, can you please keep them safe just a little bit longer while I go and get the water for the spell?"

Taking a leap of faith Coda reached out and took Zanderley's hand. "Princess you may not know us, but we know you. Jaz is the little dragon that was with you when you were kidnapped. Jewel was the little pixie that followed you to let your sisters know where to find you. I am the dragon guardian that oversaw making sure you were safe. I know I failed because you were kidnapped but I have been fighting to find you. I am also the blue dragon that saved you from Morgana's hut. The other two lying next to your sisters are Zeke and Anton they are dragon guardians as well as your sisters' mates. Will you let me take you to the spring to gather the water?"

Zanderley just stared into his sea serpent green eyes. After a couple of minutes, she blinked and nodded. Looking back at Jewel, Jaz, and Malic she asked, "You will watch over them just a little longer?"

Giving her a big smile Jewel nodded. Turning to Coda, "Okay let's get going, I have been apart from my sisters long enough."

Coda jogged over to an open area and shifted. Zanderley just watched as this handsome man turned into the magnificent beast. Feeling the warm glow starting in her heart she rubbed the heel of her hand on her chest. Shaking her head to clear it she walked over to Coda and climbed up the wing he offered. Zanderley could feel every muscle in Cody's body tremble. Not being able to resist the urge any longer she leaned forward and stoked a hand down his neck causing him to shiver. Coda tuned his head and looked back at her and asked, "Are you ready, Princess?"

Startled Zanderley's body jerked and asked, "How are you talking to me?"

"I can communicate with you telepathically. Just like you can do the same thing when you are in tiger form. You can talk to any dragon, shifter, or human you have a bond with."

"Then why can I talk to you? I do not know you. How do we have a bond?"

"How about we talk about that when we know each other better? We need to focus on waking your sisters and their mates."

Nodding in agreement she held on the best she could when Coda took flight. Zanderley looked at the land and wondered what it looked like before the curse. Without thinking she spoke to Coda telepathically, "Do you think that my sisters are strong enough to save our uncle, beat Morgana, and save our realm?"

"Yes, Princess I do. I have seen your sisters do some remarkable things so far. Now that you will be with them, I know you three will be unstoppable. Your sisters had been searching for you ever since you went missing. We searched all Edan for you. When we found out that Morgana had taken you from Athens, Greece, we quickly followed you here. We had to talk your sisters in to spending the night in the castle because of what lurks in the dark since the curse. The night we arrived in Aadya; Morgana's army attacked the castle. Well at the time we thought it was Kahn's army. Then the army descended on us, your sisters are truly warrior queens. Then as soon as the sun rose, they were packed telling us to hurry. Or they were going to save you without us. I can tell you want to ask something. What is it, Princess?"

"Tell me about them. What are they like? Are they snobs? Are they nice?"

"Your sisters are wonderful. Temprance is the red headed gypsy, she is funny, smart mouth, brave, and she has an excessively big heart. Now Acelyn the raven-haired beauty, she has a short fuse, wears her feelings so everyone can see them, smart mouthed, brave, and has an excessively big heart. Princess, you have nothing to fear. They will welcome you with open arms. I have watched and heard them cry because they were worried about you. They already love you."

"I am afraid they will be upset that I cast a spell to put them asleep."

"Princess, they will understand that it was for their safety."

"Okay." They flew in silence for a little while before she spoke, "Hey, Coda."

"Yes, Princess."

"You do not have to call me princess, you can call me Zanderley."

Smiling to himself he said, "It would be my pleasure, Zanderley."

Coda landed next to the spring and digging in the sack she took from Temprance she filled up a water flask. Coda watched their surroundings and noticed there was a minotaur watching them. "Zanderley, we need to go now," said Coda with some urgency.

"Why what is wrong?" Asked Zanderley looking around. "Ooohh MY!" said a surprised Zanderley as she scrambled back on Coda's back.

Just as soon as Coda took flight the minotaur lifted its huge battle hammer and charged. Coda circled then made a dive to the minotaur and sending a jet of blue flames he rendered the minotaur to ashes. Knowing that word would get back to Morgana where Zanderley was he said, "Hold on I need to get us out of here fast." Pinning the bag between her and Coda she wrapped her arms around his neck and held on.

Coda landed with a thud almost making Zanderley fall off making her scream. Zanderley clung to Coda's neck like a cat bringing her legs to lock around his neck as well.

Out of all the voices talking to her to let her know that she was safe and on the ground was Coda's. "Zanderley you are safe, we are on the ground." Opening one eye she looked at her surroundings and slowly let go. Embarrassed she said nothing as she grabbed the bag and went to her sisters and got to work.

Taking the knife out of the sack, he lifted Temprance's hand and poked her index finger causing blood to bead at the tip. Laying down the knife she lifted the bowl and squeezed two drops of blood into the bowl. She repeated the same thing with Acelyn and herself. Taking the bag of pixie dust from Jewel, she sprinkled some in the bowl. Looking at Malic she lifted the bowl so it was easier for Malic to drop a tear into the mixture. Quickly adding the water, she took the handle of the knife and stirred the mixture into a paste. Using her finger, she drew an X on her sisters' foreheads. Taking the spell out of her pocket she unfolded it, took in a deep breath, and recited the incantation.

Hail to the Gods hear my plea,
Grant me the strength I need
So that I may wake my sisters from sleep
Remove this curse that I have placed on thee
So that we may fulfill our destiny
So, mote it be.

Creating a small ball of flames in her hand she put it in the bowl, the flames turned purple with a blue glow. When the flames went out, she looked at her sisters and noticed that the X's were gone. She watched as their eyes stated to flutter. When they opened, Zanderley was met with bright violet and piercing emerald green eyes.

Chapter Thirty-Five

All Acelyn could focus on was the beautiful ocean blue eyes of her sister. There was only one thought running through her head, 'Is she real or is this another cruel trick of Morgana's nightmares?' She studied her sister, her long sun kissed blond hair was in a braid over her shoulder bringing the tail to pool in her lap. Her eyes were bright with life, but Acelyn could tell they were still a little sad with the sheen of tears in them. Sitting up, Acelyn's eyes stayed focused on Zanderley. Slowly Acelyn reached out and touched Zanderley on the shoulder. When she realized that this was real, she let out a cry and enveloped Zanderley in a hug.

Acelyn reached out a hand to Temprance, when she was close enough Temprance was pulled into the embrace with her sisters. Anton and Coda helped Zeke get to his feet then just watched the girls. He noticed that Acelyn was embracing her sisters, but her eyes were on Malic. Slowly she pulled back and stood, walking over to Malic she leaned in and kissed him on the beak. Then she asked, "If I touch you again, am I going to have more visions?" Malic shook his head keeping his eyes on is sisters. Turning to face everyone she spoke, "I have a little story for you. But first I must tell you this is our brother Malic. Our brother was killed when he was three and someone made our parents think it was our uncle."

Interrupting Acelyn, Zanderley spoke up, "It was Morgana that killed our brother. When she thought I killed you two, she told me everything she has done to our family."

Temprance grabbed Acelyn's and Zanderley's hands and the ground started to shake. Anton, Zeke, and Coda started moving towards the girls then stopped. The sky turned black as a moonless night without stars. Acelyn quickly grabbed her sisters' hands making their connection complete. The others watched as their eyes turned white and their faces turned up to the sky. Slowly they rose off the ground above everyone's heads. The wind stared to howl, and the volcano erupted. Lightning came from the gods and spun around the princesses making a vortex. When the princesses were engulfed with the electricity, they let out a scream that forced the others to shift into their dragon forms. When they were back on the ground they collapsed. Seeing that the princesses collapsed again Anton, Zeke, and Coda quickly shifted. They knelt by the princesses to see if they could wake them from slumbering once again.

Anton sat down and cradled Acelyn in his arms talking softly to her, Zeke leaned up against a tree stump with Temprance in his arms. Coda sat with Zanderley's head in his lap and was stroking her hair. Malic talked with Jaz and Jewel while he watched the dragon guardians with his sisters. Without taking his eyes off his sisters he asked, "Do you think Coda will love Zanderley as much as the others love Temprance and Acelyn?"

Looking up at the majestic bird, Jewel smiled and said, "Yes, I think he will love just as hard and true. He is a noble prince and a good man. His confidence broke when Zanderley was taken. Right now, he feels that he is not worthy of her love or trust."

"But that was not his fault, and when he was able, he looked for her. Coda also said that he was going to rescue her, and he did," said a flabbergasted Malic.

"That does not matter, Malic. Take it from me, I still feel like a failure to her because I could not save her from Kahn."

"You should not feel like that it was not your fault either. Both of you were fighting against forces that you could have never defeated on your own. You both are lucky you are alive, so give my sister and yourself a break."

One by one the princesses woke. Acelyn was the first seeing that she was in Anton's arms she snuggled in and kissed him under his jaw.

Acelyn patted Anton's chest to let him know she wanted up and said, "My sisters are still knocked out?"

"Yes, Dove," said Anton.

"They might be out for a while. I think we need to start setting up camp, it will be night soon." She turned her head and asked, "Malic, can we make camp here? Because I would rather not travel at night considering what we had to fight our first night here. We need one night of restful sleep. If my sisters are feeling the way I am, I know they need to rest."

"Yes, you may camp here. You will be safe. This place is shielded from Morgana's sight, or anything with evil intentions. If you stay in the boundaries of the Dead Lands you may roam and find supplies, if you need anything from outside the Dead Lands, I will get it. But yes, light will be fading soon."

"Okay, thank you, Brother. Will you stay the night with us?'

"If you want me to, I will stay."

"Of course, we want you to stay. Now let us get camp set up. Jaz and Jewel, will you please get some rocks and make a circle with them to contain the campfire. Malic, you stay here with Zeke and Coda to make sure our sisters are safe. Anton and I will gather some wood for the fire."

Anton and Acelyn took off to the broken-down trees, they were incredibly quiet not knowing where to start.

"So, what happened back there? Whatever happened it made all of us shift," asked Anton.

"Well, I think we got the rest of our powers."

"What makes you say that?"

"Since I woke up, I can feel the magic that I hold inside. Before I would have to concentrate on casting something," she held her palm out and fire danced, "now all I need to do is think about it and it happens." Closing her fist, the flames died out leaving a puff of smoke lingering in the air. When they made it to the downed trees Acelyn looked at Anton and smiled while she placed her hand on the tree. Walking slowly, she ran her hand down the trunk making the stone turn to dust.

Temprance was the next one to wake. Blinking her eyes, she cleared her vision and locked eyes with Malic. "We were never to find out about you, were we?"

"No, well not this soon. I was going to tell you who I was after the war was won and Aadya was safe. I have no idea what the consequences will be now that you know. That was one of the rules of me helping was not telling you or our parents."

"Why were we not allowed to know?"

"The Gods figured that you would feel the need to save me and take your focus off your destiny."

Dropping a pile of wood Acelyn said with a smile, "Well now we are going to do both. I am sure your other two sister will agree with me, we will fight anyone or anything that stands in our way of doing just that."

"I agree," said Temprance.

"Me too," said Zanderley.

All heads turned to Zanderley and her sisters smiled, "You are awake."

"Yes, and starving. I ate little when I was with Morgana. I never trusted what she gave me. So please tell me we have some food."

Smiling Jewel reached into one of the bags and pulled out a bottle and said, "And wine."

Temprance looked at Zeke and asked, "What happened to my bag?" Pulling it out from behind him he handed it to her. Standing she started to make blanket and pillow pallets for everyone to sleep on. Then she dropped down on one and patted the blanket next to her calling Zeke to join her. Acelyn grabbed Anton's hand and pulled him down on their pallet. Pointing to the one between Temprance and herself she said, "Zanderley, that one is yours."

Nodding she stood up and held out a hand for Coda to take. Looking up at her he shook his head then looked at the ground. Confused she asked, "Why are you saying no? You cannot sleep on the ground; you may share mine with me." Coda said nothing just looked at the ground. Looking to her sisters for help all they did was shrug their shoulders. It was Zeke that spoke up.

"Princess, he feels unworthy of you, he feels that he has failed you and he will distance himself from you until he redeems himself."

Stomping her foot causing Coda to look up, "Coda, that is stupid. You did not fail me; Jaz was with me when Kahn came for me. He was so powerful, and I had just gotten my powers. Even if you were there, he would have still taken me. I may not have been a part of this group for long, but I have learned a lot on my own, and one of them is that I am your Queen. So, I am saying to stop beating yourself up over something that was not your fault. Now will you share my pallet with me? You rescued me from Morgana, and I would feel safer knowing that someone is watching my back keeping me safe." She held her hand out one more time to Coda. With eyes locked on Zanderley's he reached up and took her hand. Walking over to the pallet they sat.

While the heroes ate, talked, and rested up for events to come, Morgana raged out of control destroying her hut. She tried to find the princess by sending scouts and tried to find her by looking in a bowl of scrying water but nothing. When she called on the magic of the choker, she had put on the princess, the magic did not answer back. Morgana picked up her bag she had packed and set out to find the princess that slipped through her grasp. "How did that little bitch get away? I know someone must have helped her. I think when I find her, I will have fun playing with her before I end her life."

Epilogue

Just on the edge of Singing Fields Nightwing landed and they quickly set up camp. As the group watched the sun fall and the moon rise, they never knew they were being hunted. Morgana knew she was on the trail of someone but could not see who it was. All she could see was the magic trail that was left behind. Taking the vial out of her bag she no longer cared that it was the last one of its kind. Uncorking the vial, she drank the blood of a dragon pixie.

Feeling the power flow into her she saw the shimmer just for an instance before it disappeared again. Thinking it was the princess she started her spell to make whoever was hidden visible. Kane felt the magic ripple on his skin and quickly got into motion. "Nightwing, it is not safe here; something is wrong." Kane cupped Catarina's face in his hands and spoke, "My love please do not fight me. You need to keep our unborn daughter safe, go with Nightwing and the others, I will meet up with you soon."

Feeling the danger herself, she kissed him and climbed up Nightwing's side and settled on his back. Kane lifted Norman up and handed him to Catarina. "I love you, Kane, please stay safe and come back to me," said Catarina. Kane nodded and shifted into his falcon form.

Morgana finished the spell just in time to see Nightwing lift of the ground. She conjured a fireball and threw it at Catarina. Knowing there was only one way to save his child and soulmate, Kane flew in front of the fireball rendering him to ashes. Catarina watched the whole thing as it was happening. When Kane died, she let out a scream that pieced the night. If it had not been for Ember, Catarina would have jumped off to her death to join Kane.

The End

Of

Book Two

Of

The Sisters of Aadya

Keep Reading for a sneak peek into Book Three

Thank You

I would like to thank, my loving husband, Charles Titler, for his love and support. My mother-in- law, Gloria Titler, for the help in proofreading and editing to get this book ready for the publisher. My sister, Sonya Penoes, for the unwavering confidence she has in me. My nephew, Randy Titler 2nd, for taking on the role as my publicist, I know it is not an easy job to keep me on task, but you are doing great. Dorrance Publishing for brining my stories to life so that I may share them with the world.

The Battle for Aadya
Book Three of The Sisters of Aadya

by Leigh Titler

Prologue

Thousands of years before Princess Temprance, Princess Acelyn, and Princess Zanderley were born is when the darkness started. There was a witch that lived in the forest just off the castle grounds and her name was Surana. Surana had one child, a girl, and her name was Morgana. When Morgana was fifteen her father died from sickness. Surana was lost in her grief and mourned her dead soulmate for months. Over time Surana's grief transformed her into a dark witch. Instead of using her powers to help others she used them to bring people pain and heart break that she felt.

King Alexzander 1ˢᵗ found out what Surana was doing and placed a bounty on her head. After Surana was captured she was brought in front of the King and he sentenced her to be hung and her corpse burnt by the hottest man-made fire, then for her ashes to be spread in different parts of the thirteen kingdoms. Morgana watched as her mother's sentence was carried out. She made a silent vow that she would end the royal blood line of King Alexzander 1st no matter how long it took.

Morgana ran back to the hut she shared with her mother and packed what she needed and set out for a new place to live so she could plan, knowing it would not be safe to stay around the royal estate any longer. Aadya is split up into thirteen Kingdoms; Dead Lands, Singing Fields, Firelands, Hallowed Woods, Enchanted Forest, Desiccated Woods, Emerald Sea, Black Mountains, Swamp of Broken Wishes, Dreaming Hills, Sandstorm Oasis, Lily Lagoon, and the Royal Estate.

The Royal Estate sits in the center of Aadya. Each Kingdom has their own faction and King and Queen. King Alexzander 1st's blood line is the only ones that live in the Royal Estate and they reign over all Aadya. Morgana wanted to be as far from The Royal Estate as possible, so she decided to settle down in the Desiccated Woods. Studying her mother's spell books, she searched on how to gain enough power to take down the royal bloodline. On her monthly trip to the small village outside of The Royal Estate she noticed the village people were celebrating. Walking up to a bread hawker she pulled out some silver coins and handed him the coins in exchange for the bread and asked, "What is all the celebrating for?"

"The Queen has given birth to a healthy boy; Prince Nickoli has been born."

Morgana felt the rage build, so she quickly shoved the bread in her knapsack and walked off. The hawker yelled after her, "You forgot your change, today there is no charge."

Turning around she looked at the hawker and snarled, "Keep it." Feeling the tears pool she quickly turned and walked at a brisk pace out of the village. Just on the edge of The Royal Estate where the path lead into the woods stood a creature making Morgana to slow.

The creature seemed to stand eight feet tall. His skin was black and looked like leather. He had huge bat looking wings on his back that were crimson red with black webbing. Morgana noticed that when the creature walked towards her his long claws made sparks on the rocks. His hands were bigger than her head and the nails were three inches long. He had long red and black horns that sprouted from his head. His mouth was filled with razor sharp teeth and his tongue was of a snake. When he spoke it sent fear up her spine.

"Morgana I am not from this realm, but I bring you what you seek," the creature said.

"How do you know what I seek?"

"Your dark soul speaks to me. I know you seek power enough to get your revenge for the death of your mother and to end the Royal bloodline. I will grant you this power," the creature said with an oily smile.

"I also want immortality that way I stay out of Tartus and take care of what I want."

"I think I can make that part of the deal."

"Why are you helping me? What do you get out of this?"

"I want to help you; all I want is your soul."

"My soul and that is it, what good is it doing me, plus if I give it to you, I will stay out of Tartus."

"Are you ready to make the deal?"

When Morgana nodded her head yes, the creature held out his hand palm up and with a puff of smoke a rolled parchment appeared in his hand. When he unrolled it, she looked and noticed her name on the bottom. Then she asked, "How do I sign it? Do you have a quill?"

"Hold out your hand," the creature said.

When Morgana held out her hand, he took his claw and sliced open her hand spilling her blood on the parchment making it a binding contract. The creature waived a hand over the contract, and it disappeared. Then the creature held his hand over Morgana's and sliced the palm of his hand open spilling his blood into Morgana's wound. Her blood bubbled and turned black as tar then she looked back up, she saw his eyes were deep red and they were glowing. Then she asked, "What is your name?"

The creature answered, "My name is Legion." Then he faded away, the last thing to fade was his red glowing eyes.

Morgana watched and waited for her time to strike. Years later she heard that King Nickoli and his Queen Tatianna were searching for a sorceress to help the queen become pregnant, and she knew that this was the start of her revenge. So, Morgana waited until the King and Queen were desperate for a child. When the timing was right, she sent a letter letting them know she would help. Not wanting them to know where her hideout was, she set up an illusion in the Black Mountains and waited for the King and Queen to join her.

Morgana placed the oil from a deadly night shade bloom in the elixir she gave the Queen to make the child she carried to have a black heart and help her destroy the Royal bloodline. When the King paid her two hundred gold coins, and the Queen drank the elixir, Morgana's eyes shone with triumph. Soon Morgana got word that the Queen was with child and started on the next steps of her plan. Nine months later she found out that the Queen gave birth to twins and Aadya celebrated and welcomed Prince Alexzander and Prince Kahn into the world.

She stayed close and watched the princes grow. Knowing she needed more power she searched. She found out that when done correctly you can draw the power from magical creatures when you drink the blood. When they were in their teens, Morgana sent her siren to lure Prince Kahn away, but she failed.

When the princes were of age to marry, she tried again. Morgana learned that Kahn craved power, so that is how she lured him to help her.

Together Morgana and Kahn slaughtered fire dragons and dragon pixies. The Queen and King of the dragon pixies had a child that was a fresh hatchling, her name was Jewel. Knowing their child was in grave danger they cast a spell to bind part of her powers and sent her to live with the knowledge dragon Draco. He was told not to tell her who she really was until it was safe, and she was ready to take back her throne. Morgana and Kahn killed Jewel's parents and Kahn drank the blood. Feeling powerful, Kahn returned home to his new bride and challenge his brother for the throne so he was the only king.

When he returned to The Royal Estate, he found that his Queen was missing. Returning to Morgana she filled his head with lies sealing Kahn's fate. Morgana told Kahn that the king, his own brother, killed his queen so that Kahn could never rule. So, Kahn worked on a plan to defeat his brother and take Aadya for himself. While Kahn was distracted, Morgana watched King Alexzander and Queen Anastasia. When she heard that the King and Queen was with child, she decided on how to break the bond between the brothers once and for all. In the fall the Queen gave birth to a baby boy. When Prince Malic was three, Morgana lured him away and killed the young prince and blamed it on Kahn. This severed the bond between the brothers and King Alexzander put a bounty on Kahn's head dead or alive.

Years later, Kahn and Morgana found out that the Queen was once again with child. While waiting for the time to strike they got word of a prophecy. The Queen would give birth to three girls. When they were twenty-three, they would destroy the great evil, save Aadya, and be the best Queens that Aadya had ever seen.

Knowing that his time was limited Kahn worked on a curse that would imprison everyone and everything in Aadya. Just days before Kahn cast the curse he felt when the first princess was born. It was small but there was a tremor in his heart that he had not felt in a long time. It made him think of his Queen, his Bella. Kahn decided to kill the princesses in revenge of his beloved. He cast the curse and shifted into a massive black panther and headed for The Royal Estate. When Kahn got to the gardens, he knew he was too late. The princesses were engulfed in white orbs and disappeared.

End of The Sneak Peek

For more updates you can follow me on Facebook @authorleightitler and
Instagram @leightitler
Email leightitler@gmail.com